THE LAST DISASTER

RAVAGED LAND: DIVIDED

KELLEE L. GREENE

KELLEE L. GREENE

THE LAST DISASTER

RAVAGED LAND: DIVIDED

— — — —

BY
KELLEE L. GREENE

COPYRIGHT

This is a work of fiction. Names, characters, organizations, places, events and incidents are either products of the author's imagination or are used fictitiously. Any resemblance to actual persons, living or dead, events or locales is entirely coincidental.

Copyright © 2018 Kellee L. Greene

All rights reserved.

No part of this book may be reproduced or stored in a retrieval system, or transmitted in any form or by any means, electronic, mechanical, photocopying, recording, or otherwise, without the express written permission of the author.

First Edition January 2018

MAILING LIST

Sign up for Kellee L. Greene's newsletter for new releases, sales, cover reveals and more!

Mailing list link: http://eepurl.com/bJLmrL

COMING SOON...

Book two in the Ravaged Land: Divided series is coming soon. Please subscribe to the mailing list to be one of the first to know when it's available! And follow Kellee L. Greene on Facebook.

BOOKS BY KELLEE L. GREENE

Ravaged Land: Divided
The Last Disaster - Book 1
Book 2 Coming Soon!

Ravaged Land Series
Ravaged Land -Book 1
Finding Home - Book 2
Crashing Down - Book 3
Running Away - Book 4
Escaping Fear - Book 5
Fighting Back - Book 6

The Island Series
The Island - Book 1
The Fight - Book 2
The Escape - Book 3
Book 4 Coming Soon!

The Alien Invasion Series
The Landing - Book 1
The Aftermath - Book 2

Destined Realms Series
Destined - Book 1

FROM THE AUTHOR

Dear Reader,

The Ravaged Land: Divided series is set in the Ravaged Land world, but it can be read as a stand-alone series. The Last Disaster takes place in the same world, but with different characters and at a different time.

I really hope you enjoy The Last Disaster! Thanks for reading!

Kellee L. Greene

1

There was no way to know for sure, but I'd estimated I'd been living alone for about a year after my mom died. What I couldn't figure out was why I was still alive. Somehow, I'd managed to continue to go on... I still hadn't killed myself.

The only reason, at least that I could come up with, was that I'd made a promise to the two people that had meant everything to me. My parents. But now that they were dead, I didn't know why I was so intent on keeping that promise.

My father had told me that our family was different from everyone else. We were tough. He'd say people like us didn't just give up. If my mom and dad would have given up, I wouldn't have ever been born.

Life hadn't been easy, but it hadn't been that difficult either. I'd spent twenty years or so living in the same small house, barely stepping off our front porch. I never saw the world beyond our yard. In a way, at least to me, it had felt as though I'd given up long ago.

Everything was about to change. I couldn't do it any longer. There was no way I could spend another day alone. Not to mention the fact that supplies were running low. Soon, I wouldn't have a choice about leaving. If leaving my home meant I was going to die, well, then so be it.

A few years ago, a storm ripped through the area tearing most everything down. It was a miracle that our house was still standing. Although, really, it was ready to crumble to the ground any day. The house was in such poor condition that I worried if I breathed too heavily it might collapse on top of me.

My mother and I stayed in the dilapidated building because it was fully stocked. We'd had everything we could have ever needed all in one place.

A few years before the big storm, my dad had died leaving my mom and me alone. After he passed, she hadn't ever been the same. He'd gotten sick, and there hadn't been a damn thing we could have done about it.

We'd had various limited medicines, but nothing for what ailed him. He fought hard like he had with everything, but it was one battle he couldn't win.

My parents used to tell me stories about a time when there were doctors and all kinds of different medicines. They'd told me there were large buildings that had been constructed for only one purpose, to take care of the sick, injured, and dying, but that sort of luxury no longer existed. Those times, if even real, were long gone.

Truth be told, I couldn't even comprehend some of the things she'd told me about their life before the storms. It all sounded like a fantasy tale to me.

The world outside our four walls was nothing at all like what they'd described to me. I had to stay indoors hiding from all the bad things that were lurking out there. Things that could kill me.

They told me of dangerous animals and unkind people that would take your life, just because they could. I'd never seen anything or anyone, but nonetheless, I believed them.

One of my first memories was of my dad teaching me how to protect myself. He taught me everything he could about surviving.

If I had to, I could take down a man bigger than myself. Although, the only real practice I'd had at doing that, was on my dad.

The most important thing he'd taught me, besides how to find food and water, had been how to kill. Animals. People. How to fight for my life.

My dad had told me he wished I'd never have to use any of what he taught me, but that he believed one day I would. One day, he and my mom wouldn't be around to take care of me, and I'd have to fend for myself. When he'd told me that, I was pretty sure he hadn't known just how quickly that day would come.

I stuffed the backpack with as much of the supplies

as I could. All of the necessities. Anything that would help me stay alive until I got further south. South... where it would be warmer, and I could rebuild.

The one thing I needed to make sure I didn't forget, was the gun my mom had given me the day she passed away. I looked at the black metal, pushing away the memory that was trying to overtake me. I swallowed it down with a cough and tucked the gun into the back of my pants.

There was a big part of me that was anxious to get out of the place I'd been stuck inside of my entire life. But there was another part of me that was beyond terrified.

I zipped up my jacket and glanced out the window. My mom had told me to head south. She'd echoed my dad's words and told me to never trust anyone. She'd told me to take the small bag of seeds and find a new home. Something near water and far, far away from other people.

Then she'd told me she loved me and less than ten minutes after that she was gone. Tears welled up in my eyes. I'd failed at pushing away the memory.

I couldn't let the tears fall. Not now. It was surprising that there were even any left, but I couldn't let my emotions take over. I had to leave. I had to be the tough girl my parents wanted me to be since the day I was born. They wanted me to be strong and brave like them, and that was exactly what I planned to be.

"Goodbye house," I said looking around the disaster

area I called my home. I closed my eyes and listened, hoping there would be some kind of sign that would tell me I was doing the right thing.

There wasn't anything. In fact, it was so quiet, I was pretty sure I could hear the flurries falling into the pure white, untouched snow outside.

"Well, all right then."

I checked to make sure the gun was tucked away right exactly where I wanted it and stepped out onto the porch. It wouldn't take that many steps before I was further than I'd ever been in my entire life.

I'd been born in the small house to my loving parents, and now, I was leaving the place I thought one day I'd die inside of behind. It was hard to understand exactly what I was feeling, but fear was definitely one of the many feelings.

I sighed and walked away from the house. Each step put more and more distance between myself and my home. I thought it would reach out and pull me back, but it didn't. If anything, it felt like it was pushing me away. To get out of there. To hurry.

It was like a clock was ticking and if I didn't hurry something terrible would happen. If I was quiet enough, I was pretty sure I'd hear the sounds of the ticking and the tocking.

"Come on feet," I said forcing a slight bounce in my step.

I stepped out past my yard, past an uprooted tree and looked over my shoulder. For a second, I wondered if the house might just poof out of existence. I chuckled at the thought.

I took a massive step over a thick, rotting tree trunk that was lying on its side and looked up at the sky. It only took me a second to realize which way was south. One of the many skills my dad had taught me that I hoped would be useful in my travels. Thanks, dad.

The ground was covered in at least a foot of snow, but it didn't bother me anywhere near as much as the cool air against my face did. My skin felt like it was being stung, and even though I couldn't see my cheeks, I was pretty sure they were pink.

There were so many trees that had been uprooted and blown about by the storm that had come through a couple years ago. In fact, very few were still standing. The trees were scattered across the ground, all of them pointing like gnarled fingers in different directions. The storm had been violent. It was a miracle that we had survived.

The few trees that still stood were pretty beat up. Most of them didn't stand straight, but they'd fought back against the destructive winds and tornadoes and somehow managed to hold their ground.

I needed to be like one of those trees. To be strong and stand up to even the most powerful of forces.

Even though the branches on the trees were empty, they'd survived the storms. Unfortunately, they appeared to be having a harder time battling against the long winter.

The cold and snow had eased up, but it had been years with these conditions. It was the main reason my mom told me to go south. If I could get to a warmer location, I could plant the seeds. I could start to build my own little oasis and live out the rest of my life.

But I wasn't even sure if that was what I wanted to do. Why would I want to live out the rest of my life alone?

I swallowed hard and pressed on. It was going to be a long journey, and the faster I walked, the quicker I'd get there... wherever there was.

The sun had moved across the sky much more quickly than I had anticipated it would. I wasn't about to admit it, not even to myself, but my legs and my body were not prepared for the vigorous workout.

I'd been indoors my entire life. The one thing I'd never practiced or trained for, was all the walking I'd have to do.

I yawned so big my eyes closed tightly. They popped open with my exhale, and my entire body froze at what was in front of me.

Not far ahead were two men. My dad would have wanted me to run, but I didn't. My feet felt as though they were glued to the ground watching as they threw punches at one another.

I ducked down behind a tree stump as best as I could and watched. Right when it looked like one of the two was winning, the other would land a blow.

"Don't get involved, Emery," I told myself almost silently.

The words sounded like a recording in my mind. It was definitely something my dad would have said to me.

I couldn't look away.

I wanted to know what was happening. Why were they fighting?

These two men were the first two people I'd ever seen besides my parents. I'd have been lying if I would have said I wasn't fascinated. It was so much more than that.

Curious.

Intrigued.

The desire to see their faces was overwhelming.

One of them was all marked-up with ink all over his face and neck. He slammed his fist into the other man's face, and for a second, it looked as though time stood still. Neither of them moved, but then, the unmarked man started to tip backward. He fell like a stone onto his back.

The marked-up man knelt down beside him and started going through his pockets. He pulled something out, and his eyes darted around the area before he stood. He pulled his hood over his head and turned away. Snow spat out from beneath his boots as he ran.

I still couldn't move. It was like my body forgot how to work.

I stared at the man's unmoving body lying in the

snow. My dad's voice echoed in my head, but still, I didn't heed the repeated warnings.

The poor guy was just lying there in the cold snow... helpless. What was I supposed to do?

Was he even still breathing?

He could die.

I couldn't leave. I had to try to help. When I was sure the other guy was gone, I made my way over to the man.

2

I pointed my gun at his head and looked down at him. His eyes were closed. Blood leaked out of his nostril and trickled down his cheek, into the pure white snow. By the gentle up and down motions of his chest, I knew he was still alive.

I could leave. The man wasn't dead. He'd wake up and be able to go back to wherever it was he'd come from.

His eyes opened to tiny slits, and he groaned. I could tell his eyes were focused on the barrel of my gun.

"If you're going to shoot me, just get on with it then," he said in a thick, groggy voice. "As you might be able to see, I'm in no mood for games."

I adjusted my grip on the gun and bit my lip. He snorted slightly as he forced his eyes open wider.

"Oh. Yeah. You're not going to shoot me," he said

pushing himself up into a seated position. His back was rounded, and he looked weak. He wiped his face with the back of his glove as his eyes met mine. "You're not one of them. Who are you?"

"I'm nobody. Who are you?"

"What a coincidence." He grinned. "I'm nobody too. Lots of nobodies out here these days, huh?"

He rubbed the back of his head for a few seconds before weakly slapping his hand against his chest. I watched as the blue-eyed man pounded his fist against his knee.

"Dammit!" he said patting his jacket right where the marked man had gone through his pockets. His eyes started scanning the area. "Did you see which way that bastard went?"

I nodded.

"Helpful. He took something of mine, and I want it back," the man's eyes stopped on the footprints in the snow. I watched him as he tried to get up. He stopped and pressed his hand against the back of his head. "Oww, shit that hurts!"

He looked at the fingers of his glove which were covered with even more blood. The man wiped it off in the snow in an attempt to clean it off.

"Must have hit a rock when I fell," he said, and I shrugged. He pushed himself up and planted his feet in the snow. He kept his eyes on me as he wobbled back and forth. "I'm Ryder."

I cleared my throat, parted my lips slightly, but then I hesitated. My shoulders relaxed as I sighed. "Emery."

"You're not all marked up," Ryder said. It sounded like he was asking, or maybe that he was surprised.

"Should I be?"

He shook his head, keeping his eyes locked on mine. "It wouldn't suit you."

"Why was he hurting you?" I asked, gesturing toward the footprints.

Ryder took a step closer and looked at the gun I still had pointed at him. "You can put that down. I'm not going to hurt you or anything."

"Why should I believe you?"

He smiled, but then winced as if the smallest movement had hurt his face. "I guess you shouldn't, but I really won't. If you were marked-up like that other guy, then I'd try, but you're not."

"No, I'm not."

Ryder looked me up and down. It made me feel a bit uneasy, and it seemed as if he'd noticed.

"I'm just trying to figure you out," he said.

"There isn't anything to figure out."

He shook his head, wearing a half-smile that made him look kind of cute, even with blood smeared all over his face. Not that I should have noticed. "I disagree."

"You didn't answer my question," I said as a strand of hair blew in front of my face. The wind was suddenly so brisk it felt as though it had sliced my cheek where the hair had touched it.

Ryder cocked his head to the side. "What question?"

"Why was he hurting you?"

"Where have you been?" He squinted at me. "They hate us. They want to kill us. I was lucky he was alone, or I'd probably be dead."

I shook my head. "Us?"

"Well, maybe not you, but definitely me and others like me." He seemed to be carefully studying everything about me. "You know about the war, right? You're not all marked up, so I figured you must be on our side."

I swallowed hard. A war? My parents hadn't ever mentioned anything about a war. Just bad people.

"What kind of war?"

"You really don't know, do you? Where have you been hiding for the last, oh I don't know, all your life? OK, maybe not quite that long." Ryder laughed at himself as if he'd said something funny, but the grin quickly fell from his face when he saw I wasn't joining in. He looked around. "Are you alone?"

I shrugged. His question made me feel uncomfortable. I didn't want him to know. If I had thought quicker, I would have instantly told him I wasn't.

Ryder looked at the footprints on the ground. "They call themselves The Evolved. Before the war, we were all together living in various bases working together to rebuild, but then, some of us had a change of heart."

"A change... in what way?" I asked quickly.

13

He shrugged one shoulder. "They changed their beliefs… they wanted something different."

"What kind of beliefs?" I asked.

"For the world. How to rebuild. Some of them thought they were better than others." Ryder glared at me and pressed his lips together to form a straight line. It almost looked as though he was worried he might be saying too much.

He watched me carefully as I slowly backed away from him. "Well, OK," I said looking around for the best way to disengage from the predicament I'd managed to get myself into. "I should probably get going."

"Where are you going?" he asked, but he looked as though he already knew I wasn't about to tell him.

"Just… on my way," I said. He pressed on the side of his face and wobbled slightly. "Are you going to be OK on your own?"

"Aww, you care." He grinned but slowly shook his head. "Yeah, I'm just a little dizzy, but I'll be fine. This wasn't the first time I'd taken a hit like that. Probably won't be the last either."

I grimaced. It was just more proof that my dad had been right about the world outside our home. "Try to cut back on them if you can. It looked rough."

"Will try." He stood there watching me. "All right, well, good luck to you then."

"And to you," I said waiting, hoping he'd take the

first step. I didn't want him to see which way I was about to walk for fear he'd follow me.

"You know," he said taking a small step forward. I aimed the gun at him again, and he held up his hands. "If you want... you could come with me. I have friends. A place you could go. It would be safer for you if you—"

"You said you were in a war. That doesn't sound safe to me," I blurted.

He blinked his gorgeous blue eyes at me. "No, I suppose it doesn't, but it is... at least for now."

"Thank you. I appreciate the offer, but I'm going to have to decline," I said.

He nodded and flashed me a weak smile. "I understand." He placed his hand on his chest pocket again, and his frustration resurfaced. "God dammit!"

"What did he take from you?" I asked even though I should have let the conversation end.

"My lighter."

I nodded.

My family had been lucky to have everything we'd acquired. Our supplies had been running low, and each item we had was precious. Even though I could start a fire with twigs and branches, I too would have been pissed if someone took something that belonged to me. Ryder had probably felt the same way about his lighter.

Items weren't easy to find anymore. I could still remember one time when my dad was still alive, and he'd come back from what he'd called a run. He and my mom were standing in the kitchen talking in hushed voices about how the nearest town was nearly emptied. My dad had said he might need to start venturing out further. I could still remember my mom telling him that he could, but only over her dead body.

We'd had so much back then. It was kind of an obsession of my dad's to collect as much as possible, but at least it was something that had allowed us to live rather comfortably for my whole life up until recently.

That was before everything went to crap, and now here I was face to bloody face with a man who'd been beaten for his lighter. A lighter. Things were definitely different, and not for the better.

"You sure I can't help you get to where you're going?" Ryder asked glancing once again at the footprints his enemy had left in the snow. "Those guys... they'd take you, and I really don't even want to think about what they'd do to you."

"Kill me, I'd guess."

Ryder chuckled, but it didn't sound like he actually found anything funny. "No, but you'd probably wish they would."

"Then I should probably get on my way," I said tucking my gun back into my pants.

"You're lucky you still have one of those," Ryder said flicking his fingers toward my hidden gun.

I shook my head.

"Yeah, don't see many of those around anymore."

"Oh."

"One of those is far more valuable than a lighter." His eyes were glued to my hip. He waved his hand at me and turned slightly. "I should get back too. Any longer and they might send out a search party."

"Really?" I asked.

He shook his head. "Nah. Good luck to you. Stay away from the tattooed men and women."

I bobbed my head once. "I will. Thanks for the advice."

Ryder flashed me a quick smile and wave before he walked away. He glanced back at the footprints but then kept walking in the opposite direction.

I watched him for a few minutes and then adjusted my backpack. It was time to get back on track.

No more wasting time checking on others. It would be best to keep going south and avoid everyone, just like my dad would have wanted.

3

Every so often I looked over my shoulder expecting to see Ryder chasing after me, but he wasn't there. Maybe there was a part of me that almost hoped he would come back. Although I'd been suspicious, maybe I hadn't needed to be.

He seemed nice enough, and if he would have wanted to do something to me, or take something from me, he probably would have at least tried. But even in his condition, it didn't seem as though he had any interest in stealing from me. He hadn't seemed even the least bit afraid of my gun.

Maybe he could tell I hadn't ever used it on a person. Had my hand been shaking? My whole body had probably been shaking.

Ugh.

I'd been lost in my thoughts, unsure of how far I'd

traveled when I saw the snow-covered city stretched out before me. The only reason I knew it had been a city was because there were a few buildings that were still standing. Those that had been made of brick had apparently been able to withstand the violent storms a few years ago.

Everything else that would have been in a city was gone. Buildings and homes erased away as though they'd never existed.

Anything that had remained after the storms my parents lived through must have been wiped away during the last big storm. If I wouldn't have seen pictures, I wouldn't even be able to imagine what the world had once looked like.

I wondered if my dad had come through this city years ago. Maybe he'd walked on the same space I was walking on.

Even though I would have liked to feel a connection to him, I didn't. The whole area had an eerie feeling. It was like the only thing that was still hanging around the decimated city were ghosts and spirits from a long time ago.

If my dad had come to this town, there wouldn't be anything for me to salvage. He wouldn't have left any stone unturned.

If it hadn't been for that horrible feeling in the air that someone was watching me, I would have considered going through some of the buildings that were still standing. But I just wanted to get the hell away from the ghost town so I could shake the creepy feeling.

I moved my feet quicker as I moved closer to the edge of the town. The muscles in my calves tightened with each step as if they were pulling me down toward the ground, begging me to give them a rest.

"Soon," I whispered.

With each step, I could feel my anger rising. My frustration felt as though it was trying to rip itself out of my chest. It hit me so suddenly it almost threw me off balance. I wanted to scream out my pain, but I was too scared. It wasn't fair. I shouldn't have to be doing this all alone.

My mom and dad had had each other. I had no one.

Maybe I shouldn't have ever left home. I could have just stayed there and froze to death. If that didn't do the trick, I could have always opted to use one of the remaining bullets on myself.

Hell, I could have just gone with Ryder and taken a risk. What was the worst that could have happened? He'd end my lonely, miserable life?

I shook my head at my words even though there wasn't anyone there to see. Maybe next I'd start talking to myself too. I must have been losing my mind. Or maybe I already had.

Ryder seemed like a good person, but what did I know. I didn't know shit. Nothing. I'd known two people my entire life, there was no way I could accurately judge someone's character after having known them for a few minutes.

The world I was trying to navigate on my own was an absolute mystery. The only thing I had to go on was what my parents had taught me, and I wasn't sure it was going to be enough.

I turned the corner of a brick building, tempted to take a peek inside. Every nerve ending in my body twitched as if they were afraid I might stop moving my feet.

The vast emptiness beyond the city was in full view. It wouldn't be long before the city was behind me and I would again be consumed by the desolation and loneliness of the outside world.

It could be my last chance to find a few supplies. There could have been something left behind that I could use, or maybe even something to eat.

It wasn't worth it.

Was it?

I heard a thud of boots in the snow behind me and quickly turned to look over my shoulder. There wasn't anything there. I turned back around and was face to face with a slender, scummy toothed man.

"Hello," he said, his face smudged with dirt. He wore a knit hat that had been ripped. Threads dangled in front of his smiling face.

I sucked in a sharp breath, but I didn't move. A feeling of dread set in.

"Well, now," he said through his gross teeth. "Look what I found."

I worked to control my breathing as I slid my hand around my side trying not to make any sudden moves. I needed my gun.

"Uh, uh, uh. Please don't do that," he said tapping a dirty knife at the center of my chest.

"I don't want any trouble." My voice was beyond shaky.

"No one ever does. I'd be worried if someone," he sniffed loudly, "came up to me and said 'hey, I want some trouble.' Yeah, that's definitely something that would be cause for concern don't you think?"

I couldn't say anything. I just stared into his lack-luster eyes trying to see if I could figure out exactly what he wanted from me.

"It's weird though," he said squinting at me. I could hear more boots crunching in the snow behind me. "You don't have the marks on your face."

I shook my head.

"Perhaps you have them somewhere else then," he said. His eyes brightened with excitement, and I could feel mine filling with fear. The widening grin on his face told me he knew it too.

Before I could even make a move, hands wrapped around my arms. The gross-toothed slender man jerked his chin forward, and they dragged me backward.

I tried to dig my feet into the snow to slow them,

but my feet slipped around. I couldn't get any traction. My stomach tightened into a knot, and I couldn't think straight.

My dad had prepared me for this... or at least we'd both thought he had. But it was happening, and I couldn't for the life of me, think of how to get myself out of the situation. My mind was a complete blank.

Even if I managed to get away, I was outnumbered. How far could I even get? They were holding me. I couldn't reach my gun.

They dragged me several feet away before pressing my back against what felt like a metal post. It was jagged, and I could feel the coolness through my jacket.

"Let me go!" I shouted, jerking both arms at once.

I broke free, but my feet slipped out from under me. The slender man laughed as the other two grabbed my jacket and yanked me right back up.

"Tie her up already! She's fiesty," the slender man said, all excitement gone from his eyes. It had been replaced by something darker.

One of the men held me while the other yanked off my backpack. He tossed it off to the side to free up his hands. Even though I couldn't get to it, I was thankful they hadn't taken my gun.

I jerked my arms around trying to get free, but they were quick with the rope. They worked in unison perfectly. If I had to guess, it probably wasn't their first time tying someone to the exact post I was held against.

One of the men tied my hands together in front of my body. The rope was so tight, the smallest movement made it feel like sharp blades were slicing into the skin at my wrists. I clenched my teeth and tried to hold still.

Using the same piece of rope, the same man dropped down to his knees and tied my feet together at the ankles. The other man smiled at me as he pulled out a second rope and tied it around my waist, knotting it behind my back.

I jerked forward to test the strength of the post. My body barely moved at all, and the men all looked at one another before chuckling. They were proud of their work.

"Check her pack," the slender man said as he picked at his front tooth with his fingernail.

The sound of the zipper being pulled down cut through the air. He started pulling out all of my things one after the other. My blanket was carelessly tossed into the snow, along with my change of clothes and my food.

"Good stuff in here," the man going through my backpack said.

I couldn't pinpoint my exact feeling as I stood there helplessly watching him rifle through my backpack. Terrifying. Distressing. Invasive. Furious. They sifted through my personal items, without a care. As if they had some kind of right to them.

"Why did they send you out alone? And with all this

stuff? Seems kind of foolish," the slender man said looking around. "Is this some kind of trap?"

"Yeah, it is, and if you don't give me my things back and let me go, they'll come over here and kill you," I said without giving my words any thought. It would only take seconds for them to realize my empty threat.

The slender man's eyes slowly scanned the mostly leveled city. A sinister grin sprouted on his face when he turned back to face me.

"Liar," he said stretching out the word. He took small steps making his way closer to me. I flinched as his hand jerked toward my neck. "I'm curious."

He pinched the metal tab hanging off my jacket zipper and pulled down slowly. His eyes focused on my neck.

I swallowed hard as I tried to work to get my hands free without slicing too deeply into them. The rope was just too tight. I locked my elbows and tensed my muscles as I jerked both hands upward.

My balled-up entwined fingers smacked him just above the groin. He grunted and sneered at me.

"Hold her!" he shouted, and the men instantly obeyed. They grabbed my arms and held them over my head. The slender man roughly pulled the zipper down the rest of the way. My jacket split open, and the cold air slammed into my chest.

He grabbed the hem of my shirt and yanked it up to my chin. I shivered as the cold sank through my skin and into my bones. The slender man placed his icy, dirty hand on my stomach.

"Mmm… soft. No markings though," he said grinning. He leaned closer, his lips inches from my ear. "Your skin is so smooth… so perfect."

He slid his hand higher, moving slowly toward my breast. I fought back the tears that were threating to roll down my cheeks.

"If the markings aren't up here," he said curling his fingers under the band of my bra before changing directions. His hand moved back down my stomach. "Then they must be down here."

My lungs squeezed together. It felt like I couldn't take in any oxygen. Everything around me started to swirl together. The only thing I could see was the guy's disgusting, smiling face.

"Don't. I'm not one of them," I said.

"So, you are a liar."

The man close to my backpack chuckled. "We knew that when she said they'd come for us if we didn't let her go."

"Just let me go," I begged.

He clicked his tongue and started moving his hand toward the button on my jeans. "I have to know for sure if you are one of them. Because if you are, you'll go back to them and tell them about us. And we don't want that."

"I'm not one of anyone!"

"There's only one way to know for sure," he said

popping open the button on my pants. There wasn't anything I could do to stop the single tear that leaked out of the corner of my eye. It felt like a blob of ice was sliding down my face.

"Please don't," I begged. My entire body trembled uncontrollably.

He put his hand on the zipper, but he stopped moving. The slender man blinked several times before swallowing hard. The men holding my arms suddenly let go.

"Untie her," the voice said.

4

The man on my right moved his fingers quickly in an attempt to untie me, but his nerves caused him to fumble around. Beads of sweat popped up at his temples, and he started puffing out rapid breaths. His anxiety was growing, and if he wasn't careful, he was going to hyperventilate.

"Get away from her," the voice ordered, and the sweaty man backed away.

A tall guy with eyes darker than the midnight sky stepped closer. He looked me up and down skeptically before slicing the rope with a knife.

The instant I was free I pushed the new guy with dark eyes out of my way. I grabbed my backpack and refilled it quickly. I stood up and started walking away, but before I could get far, a girl with long, snarled pigtails grabbed my arm.

"Hang on there, girly," she said with a slightly arched eyebrow.

My heart was still pounding. I took a slow breath and tried to assess the situation. *Remain calm.* My dad's words finally finding their way to me.

There were four new people surrounding the three who'd kidnapped me. Three guys and a girl holding a club with nails poking out at the end. They untied me, but they held me in place. They weren't allowing me to leave.

My situation had improved but only slightly. I just needed to get to my gun.

One of the guys had a knife pointed at the slender man's neck. The jacket. I'd seen that jacket before.

Ryder.

I glanced at the girl who was still holding my arm, and she looked down her nose at me. It almost looked as if she was holding back a sneer.

"Don't kill us," the slender man said, backing away from Ryder's blade. He grouped up with his two cowering buddies, all of them wearing the same panicked, glassy-eyed expression. Their fear of Ryder and his friends was very real.

"If we don't, you'll just turn around and do this again," Ryder said.

The slender man forced a chuckle. "We didn't know she was with you. How could we have known? She was all alone. No markings."

Ryder lowered his blade a few inches. "I feel like

29

we've already given all of you far too many chances. It's always something with you three."

"Please, another chance," the slender man begged.

"If the choice was mine, you'd be lying in a pool of your own blood," Ryder said, twirling his blade between his fingers before tucking it back into the sheath at his waist. He glanced at me, his face cleaned of the blood that had been smeared across his cheek. "Lucky for you, it's not my choice."

"Oh, thank God," the slender man said lowering his head in relief.

The dark-eyed guy that had come with Ryder picked up the rope. He and his buddy tied the three men who'd kidnapped me together.

"Wait! What are you doing?" the slender man asked, his eyes bugging out of their sockets.

"Bringing you back to Jacob. We'll let him figure it out," the dark-eye guy said in a voice that was barely audible from where I was standing.

"Oh, Christ! No!" the slender man said turning and trying to run away. His ankles had already been tied to the others, but apparently, he hadn't noticed. He fell face first in the snow, pulling the other two down with him. "I changed my mind! Kill me!"

Ryder shook his head. "If Jacob lets me, I'd be happy to do that for you. Let's go."

"Come on, princess," the girl holding me said as she tightened her grip. "Meaty. What have you been eating?"

We followed behind the two men that had come with Ryder. They were working together to pull along the slender man and his comrades with the least amount of falling as possible.

"How do you even know Ryder anyway?" the girl asked loosening her grip only slightly.

"I don't really know him," I said, my voice quieter than I would have liked.

She looked me up and down. "Guess you know him well enough for him to drag us out here to come looking for you. Lucky for you we did too."

"Is it?"

"Is it what?" Her eyes narrowed.

"Lucky."

She rolled her eyes and pressed her fingertips to her forehead near her eyebrow. "If it hadn't been for us, your pants would be around your ankles right now. Each one of them nasty-ass dudes taking a turn no doubt."

I gnawed on my cheek. The feeling of the slender man's hand on my skin came rushing back, sending a sick feeling into my stomach.

"So, um, yeah, you're welcome and stuff," she said bowing her head slightly as if she'd just completed something spectacular and was waiting for her applause.

"Thank you."

"You didn't answer me though. How do you know Ryder? I've never seen you around." Her head stayed forward, but her eyes shifted toward me for a split-second. "It's all quite suspicious."

I drew in a deep breath and swallowed. "I did answer you. I don't really know him. He was in a fight earlier, and I just happened to cross his path."

"And you're really not marked?"

I shook my head.

"Huh," she grunted.

There was a small part of me that wanted to ask why she'd made the noise, but a bigger part thought that the less I talked to her, the better off I would be. She didn't seem to like me any better than the slender man had. The fewer interactions I had with her, the happier I'd be.

I let out a soft sigh as I looked off toward the south. I was going the wrong way. Miss Pigtails tightened her grip again. "Don't even think about it."

"Oh, no. I wouldn't dare."

Ahead of us, Ryder said something I couldn't make out to the other two guys before jogging back to me and Miss Pigtails. "Go lead the way," Ryder said, staring at his friend's hand that was wrapped around my arm. "I need to talk to Emmy."

"Emery," I corrected.

"Emery?" Miss Pigtails said, barely able to hold in her laugh. "What kind of name is that?"

Ryder glared at her before turning and bowing his head in my direction. "I kind of like it."

"You like it so much you couldn't even get it right?"

Miss Pigtails said with a laugh. She was quickly silenced by the look on Ryder's face. Her fingers released my arm, and I sucked in a breath as if her grip had somehow stopped me from breathing in deeply. "I'll go lead the way."

"That's a great idea," Ryder said, waving her away. The second she was out of earshot he smiled. "Charlie is a bit rough around the edges."

"No? Really? I didn't get that at all from her."

Ryder laughed. "I apologize if she said something stupid or insulting or whatever."

"I don't think you can apologize for someone else."

"Oh, but I can try. It's not like I'd want you to get the wrong impression about us. We're the good guys." Ryder lifted his palms up and shrugged.

I chewed my lip for a second. "It doesn't really matter what I think."

"I think it does."

There was a long pause, but I could tell there was something he wanted to say. For some reason, he was hesitating.

I cleared my throat. "How did you know where I was?"

"I followed you." He didn't sound even the slightest bit embarrassed, or worried about how I might react by sharing that information with me.

"Why?" I asked, looking at his cleaned-up profile.

He shrugged. "It's not a safe place out here all by

yourself, and I just wanted to make sure you got on without a hitch."

"How long were you going to follow me?"

"Maybe to your destination." He turned and flashed me a smile. His teeth were white and clean.

"I doubt that."

He brushed his hands together before tucking them into his jacket pockets. "So, you should know who we are."

"You already told me before. You're on one side of some war. It's not my war. I don't need to know any more than that."

"It's everyone's war. If you live on this planet, it's your war too." He stared at me for a moment. "Anyway, That's Eli," he pointed to the tall one with dark eyes, "and that's Logan."

Even with his jacket covering him, Logan looked as though he was composed of eighty percent muscle. If he had to, he could probably wrangle the slender man and his two men all by himself.

"And you've met Charlie," he said.

"What did you tell them?"

"About what?" he asked.

I readjusted my hat. "About me. Why did they come out here and help you look for me?"

"They're my friends. We all live together. That's kind of what I wanted to talk to you about."

I shook my head vigorously. "I don't want to get involved in your war."

"Everyone's war."

"It's not mine."

He sighed. "I want you to come back and just see what we have. You don't have to stay."

"You want to bring me to your leader... Jacob." I pointed at the slender man. "He doesn't seem to like Jacob, so I'm not sure I should either."

"Jacob just doesn't like when the people he allows to leave the group continue to get in the way. Or if, like in your case of what they were doing to you, make things worse." He nodded at the stumbling men. "And they are always getting in the way and making things worse."

"If they aren't part of your group, how exactly do they fit into your war?"

"Everyone's war."

I rolled my eyes.

Ryder cleared his throat. "We call them natives. I guess technically you'd be a native too."

"What do you mean by a native?"

"A native is a person that isn't taking sides. Or like you, someone that doesn't want to participate in the war... someone that wants things to go back to how they were before The Evolved tried to take over."

I wasn't exactly sure how I wanted things to be. How could I know when I wasn't even really sure how things had been? I wanted things to go back to how they were when my parents were still alive, but that wasn't an option.

"What's Jacob going to do to me?" I asked. "I mean, since he doesn't like natives."

"He doesn't have a problem with natives as long as they mind their own business. Most of the people roaming about, not that there are many, are out there because Jacob let them go."

I shook my head. "Why would he do that? You have fewer people in your war. Isn't he afraid they'll join up with The Evolved?"

"The Evolved would probably just kill or torture them. Jacob doesn't believe people should have to fight for something they don't believe in."

"So, he just lets them go?"

Ryder nodded. "Yup. I mean he doesn't give them any of our supplies, or anything. Every man for himself and all that."

"Then he'll let me go?"

"Yeah, of course."

"OK," I said sucking in a quick breath.

Ryder turned and smiled at me. "But I bet he's going to be just as fascinated by you as I am."

"Oh, please."

"No really. I can't even remember the last time we found a true native. Maybe you're the last one." He jabbed his elbow into my arm lightly.

"Do you have markings?" I asked, my voice quiet.

Ryder's eye shifted down towards the snow. He exhaled slowly. "We all have markings. Once upon a time, we were one big happy family—"

"How big?"

"Big enough." He looked at me, but I didn't react. Ryder cleared his throat and continued. "We were all given a marking because we were all devoted to the same cause. I was given mine at birth. Those other guys, the ones that call themselves The Evolved, they have extra markings. To them, they are like badges."

My head bobbed up and down rapidly. "On their face. No mistaking them. Like the one that attacked you."

"That's right. They are proud of who they are, and they know they are strong." His shoulders dropped as he released a big breath. "They don't let people go like Jacob does. Instead, they collect people. Keep them as prisoners. Slaves."

I shook my head. "That guy fighting you... he didn't take you for his prisoner."

"He was alone. If there had been another, I'd be gone. Maybe even dead."

"Dead?"

"I'm not afraid to fight back. I don't really take orders," Ryder said raising his eyebrow at me. "I'd cause too many problems for them. They wouldn't want to deal with me."

I swallowed down the sour taste at the back of my throat. I wanted to take a drink from my water bottle, but I was afraid to stop and take it out. After Ryder's story, I just wanted to keep moving.

"I'm a fighter," Ryder said stiffening his jaw. "And it'll do you good if you become one too."

"Who said I wasn't one?"

He eyed me, but his expression didn't change. "I hope that's true. Not much longer until we're home. I think you're going to like it."

Ryder smiled as he nodded at the stretch of land in front of us. All I saw was snow for as far as I could see.

He ran ahead of us and stomped his boot on the ground in a particular rhythm. In seconds a square door opened revealing a secret underground passage.

What had I gotten myself into?

5

E li and Logan led the slender man and his buddies down into the secret underground hideaway. Charlie held the door open with one hand while she swung her spiked club with the other. She looked both bored and menacing at the same time, and I was pretty sure she knew it.

I hesitated for a second before stepping down onto the first rung of the ladder. Charlie's lip curled at one end, and she raised her eyebrow at me.

"Aww, are you scared, girly?" she said, her expression changing into a frown when she caught Ryder's chastising eyes. "What?"

"Knock it off already," he said through his teeth.

She shrugged, as her gaze shifted out toward the horizon. "Whatever."

I stepped off of the ladder and turned around. There was a long corridor in front of me. It must have been the basement of a rather large building that no longer existed.

The walls were covered with a dark, gritty scum. It seemed like the walls and the ceiling were constructed of thick concrete. I lightly touched the surface with my glove, but it didn't leave a mark in the grime. The gunk must have been there for so long that it had become part of the wall.

"Go on," Ryder said with a smile. "I know it doesn't look the best, but it's safe. It'll be OK."

He lightly put his hand on my shoulder, and I flinched. "Sorry."

Charlie hopped down off the ladder and chuckled as she walked past us. "Have fun kids," she said as she waved a strange flourish. "Enjoy your stay."

"Sorry about that," Ryder said when she was out of earshot.

"She really doesn't like me."

"She really doesn't like anyone."

I shrugged my shoulders. "She seems to like you just fine."

"Today," Ryder said, taking a step in front of me. "This way."

Our feet padded softly against the dirt-coated tile floor. Each step sounded like a muffled bass drum echoing around us.

"What is this place?" I asked.

"I think it was a school basement once upon a time." Ryder shrugged. "At least that was Jacob's guess.

I'm not sure any of us really know, but it keeps us safe."

"Is this where you stayed during the storms?"

Ryder shook his head. "Even longer than that. We found this after the war started. It wasn't too long after that they unleashed the storm."

"They unleashed the storm?"

Ryder nodded.

"Where are they now... the, I forget what you called them?" I asked as I looked up at the ceiling that seemed just as scummy as the walls and floor.

"The Evolved?"

I looked down at my feet. "That's right. Where are they hiding?"

"They don't feel the need to hide," Ryder said turning into a room at the end of the long corridor. "They roam around killing and collecting. Bring what they gather back to their bases."

"Killing and collecting what?"

Ryder cocked his head to the side and stared at me. "People. Well, and other things they might find useful. You know, supplies and stuff."

"Oh."

"That's one of the reasons I went out after you. You could have walked right into them." Ryder nodded at a long folding table with several chairs around it. "Have a seat."

He pulled out a chair for me and sat down in the one just to my right. I brushed off the mostly clean seat

41

and took off my backpack. My fingers gripped the straps tightly as I sat down.

"If you go out there alone, they'll find you. Your gun isn't going to do much good against a group of five, ten, sometimes even more." He glanced down at my hip even though my clothing covered the gun. "How many bullets do you even have left? Where did you get it?"

"It was my dad's."

"Sorry," Ryder said, fully understanding the fact that my dad was no longer with me.

I forced a tight-lipped smile. "It's fine. It was a long time ago."

"I see. I don't even know who my dad is," Ryder blurted. He snickered to himself before shaking his head. "I have no idea why I said that."

I shrugged. It didn't matter to me that he didn't know or that he told me. Everyone had a story, and I was kind of intrigued to hear more of his.

Out of the corner of my eye, I saw someone step into the room. My eyes shifted over, but I kept my head facing Ryder.

The man I assumed was Jacob walked into view, his face completely unreadable. He had a long, bushy beard that almost touched his chest and deep wrinkles at the corner of his eyes. His gray eyes revealed that he'd seen a lot... a lot more than I could even imagine.

He was probably around the same age as my dad would have been if he were still alive.

"This her?" he asked, and Ryder nodded.

"Girl, where you from?" he said, his voice hard and raspy.

I drew in a slow breath. "I'd rather not say exactly. My family hid somewhere safe for years."

"And where are they now?" he asked looking over my shoulder as if they might just pop out and surprise him.

"They're both dead."

"I see. You're all alone then, that right?"

I nodded once.

"Have any other folks come around and talked to you?" he asked as he sat down and leaned forward. He peered into my eyes as if they would tell him more about me than I could ever reveal about myself. And maybe that was true. "I'm going to assume they haven't since you're still alive and roaming about."

"No. No one else has talked to me."

The man turned to Ryder. "Have you talked to her about them?"

"Yes, Jacob, I have, but I don't think she understands the severity of the situation," Ryder said, glancing down at my bouncing knee. His hand jerked out and pressed down. "No one is going to hurt you here."

I smiled, but it quickly faded. The second he removed his hand from my leg, it started bobbing up and down again.

"OK, girl, here's the deal," Jacob said pressing his palms down against the table. His hands were covered in dirt and his knuckles puffed up like they'd been stuffed with rocks.

I shook my head. "I don't need to know any kind of deal. I just want to be on my way."

Jacob looked at Ryder, his eyes filled with confusion. "You're more than welcome to stay here. No one will lay a hand on you. I swear it to you."

I looked at Ryder out of the corner of my eyes. Apparently, it hadn't taken long for word to get to Jacob about what those men had done to me.

"You'll be safe here… for now."

"I don't like the whole 'for now' part," I said, my chair skidding backward slightly as I stood.

Jacob stood up and held out his hand. "Good luck to you then. Show her the way out."

After we shook hands, Jacob left the room without a second look. It was clear that if a person didn't want to stay, Jacob wasn't going to force them to.

I pulled my backpack on and looked up at Ryder. "Thank you for saving me, but I really should get going."

His head bobbed once. "Yeah, of course."

I nodded toward the door. "I remember the way. See you around."

"I doubt that," Ryder muttered.

My eyebrows shot up toward my hairline, and I walked toward the door. It felt like so much of my day had been lost. I really needed to get out there and move my feet to make some progress.

My feet moved rapidly down the corridor. I tried not to look into the open doors, but I couldn't seem to stop myself.

Each room was filled with people who looked back at me before returning to whatever it was they were doing. There had to be at least thirty people gathered in each room I looked in, if not more, and I hadn't looked in them all. Jacob had built himself a nice little army.

At the last doorway on my right, a delicious scent made its way into my nostrils. It was so enticing I stopped in my tracks to look inside the room.

There was a little stove with a thin tube that led up and through the ceiling. Rows of tables made perfect lines, and each chair was filled with a person that didn't seem to notice the strange girl staring at them.

"Hungry?" Ryder said, stepping up next to me. He was grinning. "Yeah, you look hungry all right."

I swallowed down the saliva that had started to wet the inside of my mouth. No matter how badly I wanted to hide it from him, my eyes and rumbling stomach gave me away.

"I think we're having beans, maybe some rice. Every once in a while, they pop up some popcorn. That's a real treat let me tell you."

"Maybe I could stay for one meal," I said softly licking my lower lip. "Jacob wouldn't like that though I'm sure."

"Let me worry about Jacob," Ryder said grabbing my hand and pulling me into the room.

He walked up to the table near the stove and filled up a plate. Ryder started walking away but turned back when he noticed I wasn't following him. He grabbed my hand and led me to an empty chair.

I watched him as he set down the food and kicked out the chair. "Go on, sit."

"Don't you want any?" I asked.

"I'll get some later. You first."

I took off my backpack and looked around the room suspiciously. No one seemed to care about me or my backpack.

There wasn't a single eye in the room on me until I noticed her staring at me. The room was dark except for a few candles placed on the tables and the flame glowing in the stove, but I'd recognize those eyes anywhere. Her glare was unmistakable.

Charlie rolled her eyes and pretended to turn back to her food. She laughed loudly at something one of her dinner companions said.

I sat down and tucked my backpack between my legs. The second the food touched my tongue, I didn't stop shoveling the warm meal into my mouth. Apparently, I was hungry. All those snack bars and watered-down oats kept me fed, but this was something different. It tasted amazing.

Ryder sat down next to me and watched me eat. I

glanced up at him after I was finished and tossed my plastic fork on the empty plate.

"It's rude to stare at someone while their eating," I said.

"Only when they eat?" Ryder said with a laugh. "Hell, I didn't even know anyone was still minding their manners."

I shrugged. "I guess I was taught to."

"We weren't all that lucky. I was raised much differently. Fall in line, or get out of the way of the guy that will. Fight for what you want if you want to survive."

"We shared. We had enough, well, up until the end." I cocked my head to the side. "I was still taught to fight to survive."

Ryder stood up and grabbed my plate, tossing it into a black plastic bag inside the tall barrel behind us. "Well, no one out there is going to give two shits about you. Don't be polite. Don't be fooled into a false sense of security if you want to survive because if you want to make it, you're going to have to be rude. Mean, even." He pointed to the door. "There's a war going on out there whether you like it or not. Don't ever forget that."

"You kind of sound like my dad."

"Your dad sounds like he was a smart guy."

I pressed my lips together hard. "He was."

"Just be tough, and don't be afraid to use," he leaned close and whispered, "that gun."

"I'm not."

Ryder looked around the room. "Sure, you won't stay with us?"

I smiled and shook my head. "Sorry."

Ryder walked me over to the ladder and climbed up, opening the door at the top. The sky was a dark shade of blue, somehow it was almost nighttime.

"Ryder?" I said tapping my fingers against the side of the ladder.

"Yeah?" he said closing the door slightly to look down at me.

I bit my lip, and I could feel the tension in my wrinkled brow. The thought of being out there alone after what happened earlier made me a little nervous. "Maybe just one night."

Ryder closed the door and hopped down off the ladder. He tried to hide his smile but failed miserably.

"Good," he said, nodding down the corridor. "I'll let Jacob know."

I hugged myself and followed him down the hall.

6

———————

At night everyone broke off into what appeared to be assigned rooms. Jacob had told Ryder to keep an eye on me, but I don't think anyone really suspected that I was secretly a spy for The Evolved.

I sat next to Ryder with my back against the cool wall. The room we were in had a single glowing candle placed on the floor in the doorway.

Every few minutes a pair of guys would walk past the door completely in sync. They moved up and down the hall, looking into the rooms. Each of them carried a gun with a long barrel that looked like it could do some major damage. Apparently guns weren't all that rare.

I was surrounded by more people than I had ever imagined were still out there, yet I felt incredibly alone. It had been quite some time since my mom had passed away, and even longer since my dad, but God, I missed them.

I needed them. I wasn't even sure if I could do this alone. It didn't matter how much training my dad had given me, all if it went out the window when I had to walk away from my home. Or maybe it hadn't ever been there in the first place, and I only first realized when I left.

I wiped the corner of my eye with the back of my hand.

"You OK?" Ryder asked leaning forward trying to look into my eyes.

"Yeah, I'm fine." I forced a smile but kept my head down. If he saw into my eyes, he would have instantly realized that I, in fact, wasn't fine.

I'd never been good at hiding my emotions. My heart was on my sleeve, and that was probably why I should have stayed home. All it would have taken was one bullet to end it all. Then I could have searched for my parents in the afterlife. If there was an afterlife.

"Maybe you should get some sleep," Ryder said, nudging me lightly with his elbow. "I'll stay awake... I mean, if you want me to watch over you."

"You don't need to. This is your home." I frowned, but he couldn't see it. "I shouldn't even be here."

He shook his head. "You're welcome here. It's just that you don't want to be here."

"I don't think I want to be anywhere," I muttered.

Ryder shook his head. I could tell he wanted to say something, but that he didn't know what to say. How could he? He didn't know me or what my life had been like.

"You need rest. You'll feel better after you get some sleep," he finally said after a long pause. He patted the ratty pillow tucked behind my back. "I'll make sure nothing happens to you. Not that anything would here."

"Nothing has ever gone wrong down here?" I drew in a deep breath and laid my head down on the pillow. My fingers held onto my backpack as if it were the only thing keeping me afloat in a sea of uncertainty.

Ryder crossed his arms and stretched out his legs. He looked down at me and our eyes locked.

I wanted to dislike him, but there was something in his eyes that grabbed me and wouldn't let go. Ryder wasn't as cold as everyone else seemed to be. If he were, he wouldn't have gone out looking for me.

"Just a few personal fights. Jacob would kick out anyone who even thought of doing anything wrong. He thinks of us as one big family, and we take care of our own."

A small smile stretched across Ryder's lips. He picked at a fingernail and pressed the back of his head against the wall.

"One really big family," I said, yawning loudly. There was no denying I was tired.

"A big, slightly dysfunctional family," Ryder said taking in a deep breath. "Sleep well."

I nodded and reluctantly closed my eyes. My first

day on my own hadn't gone at all according to plan. Hopefully, it was just a rocky start, and all the rest of my travels would go much smoother.

———

I spent another day in the underground town with Ryder and his friends. For some reason, I just hadn't been able to make myself leave.

They talked freely around me even though I kept quiet most of the time. I wasn't sure why but they didn't seem to distrust me. They made me feel included.

Charlie teased me for carrying my pack with me everywhere. She'd told me that no one would steal my 'little pack of goodies.' Supposedly, they had more stored up than I could possibly imagine. Little did she know I could imagine a lot.

With all the people living underground, they must have had an entire room filled with supplies. I wondered if they were still finding more out there. If they could, then I could too.

Then again, I could trap animals or catch fish. My dad had even taught me how to forage for certain things, although, that was nearly impossible with the cold air and snow-covered ground. There just wasn't much of anything growing, but hopefully, that would change as I went further south.

I ate dinner that night with Ryder, Logan, and Eli.

Charlie didn't sit with us. She claimed she had something she needed to do, but when Ryder asked her what it was, she just shook her head and walked away.

"Did you get enough?" Ryder asked as he, Eli and Logan sat down at the table across from me.

The room was dark, but the light danced across their faces. They didn't really smile much, and Logan quite possibly never smiled at all. They stared at me while they spooned mushy beans into their mouths.

"Yes, I did. Thanks again," I said as the three of them nodded almost simultaneously. "Have you guys known each other a long time then?"

Ryder nodded. "We all pretty much grew up together. Charlie too."

Eli chewed while he looked around the room. He swallowed the food down in one big gulp. "A lot of us did in fact. How about you?"

"I'm not from around here," I said my nerves prickling in my arms. I hated talking about myself and my life. If I talked about it, then I'd remember my parents.

"A mystery," Logan grunted.

I shrugged. "Not really… just not much to tell."

"Have you given any more thought to staying with us?" Ryder asked quickly. I was pretty sure he'd noticed the conversation had started to make me feel uncomfortable. Little did he know talking about staying, or where I was going, would also make me feel uncomfortable.

"No need. I really need to be on my way. I've spent

far too much time here already." I filled my mouth with a forkful of beans.

"Where are you headed?" Eli asked, his eyes on his plate.

I chewed on my lip for a second. "Further south."

"I've heard it's not any warmer down there," Eli said. "Is that why you're going?"

"Yes," I answered sharply.

"Warm enough down here," Ryder said without looking up.

Eli elbowed Logan. "Isn't that sweet?"

Logan's eyes quickly darted over at Ryder. "He's right though."

"I appreciate the offer guys, I really do, but I can't stay."

"There are a lot of bad guys out there. Guys much worse than the three you faced the other day," Ryder said keeping his voice low.

"I can take care of myself," I said balling up my fists tightly on my lap. Each nerve twinged and sparked, and it felt like the odd sensation was spreading down toward my legs.

All three of the guys looked up at me. I could see the concern in their eyes.

"I can take care of myself too," Logan said tossing his white plastic fork onto his empty plate. "But if three or four of The Evolved grabbed me, it's over for me. Sometimes it doesn't matter how prepared you are."

Ryder looked at me as I stood up. It seemed like he wanted to say something to stop me, but he didn't.

I picked up my plate and walked between the tables toward the trash. Jacob was walking toward me heading in the opposite direction. He kept his eyes on mine as he drew nearer.

When we were just about side by side, he nodded slightly. If he would have been wearing a hat, I imagine he would have tipped it in my direction.

I flashed him a tight-lipped smile. Jacob seemed as though he was very rough around the edges, like every wrinkle on his face had a story to tell, but still, for some reason, I liked him.

As I made my way out of the room, I could feel their eyes on me. It was almost as if I could even hear their whispers. They were probably wondering why I was going. And why it was so damn important.

I could imagine every question that was spinning through their heads, right until I walked out of the room. Inside the hallway it was quiet.

I made my way back to the room I'd slept in the previous night. Even though there weren't many in the room with me, I could hear the voices asking all the questions again.

I had to go.

I had to get out of this noisy place before I forgot the answers to the questions.

No more excuses. In the morning, I'd be back on my way.

7

I looked up at the sky to confirm the direction I want to travel. Ryder methodically walked around the area scanning the snow for footprints.

"Are you sure about this?" Ryder asked just before he got down on his knee to look closer at something on the ground.

"Positive," I said, hoping my tone would convey that I desperately wanted him to stop asking. Everything they had was very nice, and it was actually kind of good to be with others, but my mind was made up. I didn't want to be part of the war, and I wanted to finish what I set out to do.

Ryder stepped in front of me and looked down into my eyes. Warmth filled my cheeks.

"I guess this is goodbye then," he said.

"I guess so." I forced a smile. "Thanks again for everything. Especially the whole saving me thing."

"Yeah, of course," he said swallowing hard. "I just hate the thought of you out there. Next time I won't be there to save you."

"Try not to think about it," I said without blinking.

Ryder looked down at his feet. "That's going to be hard to do."

"You'll manage."

Ryder gazed into my eyes as if he was looking for something. He sucked in a deep breath and stuck out his hand.

I took off my glove and shook his hand. I wasn't sure if it was the human contact or the burst of cold air against my skin that made me shiver.

"Take care out there," Ryder said, still holding my hand.

"I will," I said, unable to look away from his eyes. "Be safe. I won't be around to help you either, you know, the next time you fight with one of those marked-up guys."

He grinned and shook his head slowly. I'd miss his smile. "I'll definitely be more careful. I doubt there are any other beautiful women out there lurking in the shadows waiting to rescue me."

I could feel the heat pump out of my chest and up to my cheeks at his compliment. My mouth felt dry. I'd be lying if I said Ryder wasn't extremely gorgeous because he was. There probably wouldn't be anyone else like him out there, but it didn't matter.

If I didn't make my feet move at that moment, I

wasn't sure if I ever would. I dropped Ryder's hand, and my fingers instantly felt cold.

My breath was icy in my chest, but I stepped away from him, waved, and forced my feet to move. I put my glove back on, and I didn't turn back.

I walked.

I hadn't made it more than roughly a quarter mile before I heard a voice behind me. Fear kept me from looking over my shoulder.

I could tell by the increasing volume of their voices that they were getting closer. The sounds were cheery. If someone had been sneaking up on me to do me harm, they would have been quiet and not so... obvious.

"Emmmmm-mmmmery," A voice from behind me sang out.

I glanced back, narrowing my eyes when I saw them approaching. What the hell?

Eli and Logan were walking just slightly behind Charlie who was casually swinging her club back and forth. Ryder was leading the way wearing a half-smile.

"What are you doing?" I called out to them.

Charlie turned to Eli and mumbled something I couldn't make out at my distance. Ryder's head jerked to the side, and I could only imagine the look he'd flashed her.

"We couldn't let you go alone," Ryder said.

I sighed and paused to let them catch up. Why were they doing this? I had to send them back.

"Keep moving," Ryder said, stepping up next to me. "Don't want to slow you down."

I shook my head. "I don't understand... did something happen?"

Ryder kept his eyes forward. "I told Jacob I needed to go with you. He wished me well, and of course, these yahoos saw me leaving and wanted to tag along. How could I say no to those faces?"

"You guys should go back," I blurted out.

"Told you," Charlie said, turning on her heel. Logan grabbed her arm and spun her back around.

"Listen to her," I said mostly through my teeth. Apparently, the dislike had become mutual.

Ryder grabbed my arm and yanked me to a stop. He placed his hands on my shoulders and looked into my eyes.

"Do you really think we want to die in the war?" Ryder asked. "We have just as much of a right to take our chances out here as you do."

"But you can do that on your own. You don't need to follow me. I have no idea what I'm doing out here. You're better off staying with Jacob or going off on your own. I don't want to feel responsible for what happens to any of you." I shrugged my shoulders to break free of his hold.

"Let her go, Ryder," Charlie said as I walked away. I couldn't help but roll my eyes even though my back was to them. "She doesn't care about you, or anyone else for that matter."

I heard footsteps moving quickly behind me. Ryder popped up at my side in an instant, startling me even though I knew someone was coming.

"We can help each other," Ryder said. "Our chances are better together. Once you get where you're going, we can leave you, but let's travel together until we get there."

It was just talk. I didn't understand why he was so adamant about traveling with me. It wasn't like they were any safer with me.

"Your chances will be better back there with Jacob."

I wanted to tell him that I didn't care what happened to me, but that I didn't want anything to happen to them. If I should die in my travels so be it.

I could see Ryder shaking his head out of the corner of my eye. "That's simply not true. We're outnumbered. I believe everything Jacob is fighting for, but I don't want to die, and I definitely don't want to end up doing God knows what for The Evolved. Please. Let us come with you." Ryder forced a smile as he blinked his eyes. "We can make our own way in this world, just us."

"I thought you said you were going to go off on your own once I reached my destination?"

"Whatever you want. Please?"

I sucked in a deep breath and stopped walking. It was probably going to be a huge mistake, but there really wasn't much I could do to stop them. They could just follow me for as long as they wanted and there wouldn't be a damn thing I could do about it. I might as well, just suck it up and agree to let them come with.

My dad would not have approved, but maybe being with them was better than the life of solitude I was heading for. Perhaps he would have understood.

"She doesn't even want to be here," I said with a groan.

"Deep down she does, or she wouldn't have come with."

"She'd do whatever you do. They all probably are," I said lowering my voice.

Ryder shook his head. "We'd talked about leaving before. Going off on our own. Seeing you doing it struck a nerve. Jealous maybe. Instead of sitting around wondering, we want to go with you."

"If anything happens to any of you, it'll be because of me."

"This is one hundred percent our choice." The corner of Ryder's mouth was curving slightly. He could tell he'd already won. "Pretty please?"

I sighed and kicked the snow. "It's a terrible, terrible idea."

"That's a yes then, right?"

My shoulders dropped down. "I can't stop you, can I?"

Ryder waved back at his friends to follow and leaned closer. "Not really."

Together, as a big group, we started walking south.

For the most part, they were quiet, leaving me a lot of time to reflect on my thoughts and choices.

I could hear my dad's voice in my head telling me I was making a mistake. Trust no one, his words echoed over and over in my mind.

If this was how I met my end, then at least I would be with my parents again. The others would probably get bored soon and go back in no time. Maybe they just had to get it out of their system. They'd probably felt trapped living underground for as long as they had. A little adventure and before long, they'd head back to Jacob.

"So, how far are we going?" Eli asked. I saw Ryder's head jerk back toward him. "Not that it matters of course, I was just wondering."

"As far south as I need to. You guys are welcome to stop whenever you want," I said without turning around.

Charlie chuckled. "She doesn't even know where she's going."

My head whipped back sharply. "I never said I did. I told you to go back. You don't have to follow me. I'm definitely not making you."

"Geez, he was just asking," Charlie said shifting her eyes away. She blinked several times as if her long lashes were trying to wave me away.

"I'll know it when I get there," I said, but it wasn't loud enough for anyone to hear. Maybe I'd only said it for my sake.

We walked for several hours before my calves were burning. I couldn't tell them though. Charlie would make some comment that would annoy me, and I definitely wasn't in the mood.

Ryder looked at me and then down at my legs. His eyes focused on mine for a few seconds as if he was trying to read my mind.

"When can we stop for a rest? Maybe eat a little something?" Ryder asked.

Maybe he had read my mind. Or maybe the way I was lifting my legs as if they were made out of metal had been a dead giveaway.

"Whenever you guys need," I said, but the slow blink that followed my words was filled with obvious pain. Anyone looking at me would have been able to tell how uncomfortable I was. Thankfully, the only one looking at me had been Ryder.

"I need one," he said. "How about over there? We can build a little shelter with some of that debris."

I nodded. I couldn't even speak because if I had, everyone would know, how weak I was.

8

Charlie sat in the snow about ten feet away from me watching the guys build a little shelter with whatever they could find. It wouldn't be warm, but we'd build a fire which would help to some extent.

There weren't any houses or secret underground rooms where we were. Ryder and his friends were doing the best they could with what was at our disposal.

They'd gathered up boards, twigs, and branches that were scattered about. One of them tied up their blanket to the top of their structure to act as our roof.

My calves were buried in the snow, but it didn't seem to be helping my sore muscles. Even though I hadn't had a choice, I wasn't ready for all of this. My body couldn't take it, and I didn't think I'd even traveled all that far from home.

Ten miles?

Fifteen?

Maybe twenty at best.

If I had stayed at home, I would have eventually run out of food. I would have died from the cold. I listened to my mother and headed south... but maybe I shouldn't have.

"Come on over. Give it a try," Ryder said waving his hand at me.

Eli and Logan were on their knees trying to get a fire going. Charlie hopped up and quickly made her way over to the shelter. She plopped down inside, staking her claim on the spot in the far left corner.

"Need help?" I asked, glancing at Eli.

"We'll get it, thanks."

"OK, but that wood looks a little too wet." If there was one thing I could do well, it was start a fire. My dad had me practice all the time.

Logan turned his head slowly and looked up at me. I bit my lip as he stared.

"Want to give it a shot?" Logan asked, saying each word slowly. It was almost as if it were a challenge.

"Sure," I said reaching into my front pocket. I clicked the lighter several times before the flame started to glow. It took a few seconds, but when the small branch caught fire, I smiled. "There you go."

"Well, that's cheating," Logan said smiling mostly with his eyes.

My grin quickly turned into a frown when I tucked the lighter back into my pocket. "It's not going to last much longer. The fluid is running out."

Logan nodded. "That's why it's good to know how to do it the old-fashioned way."

"I know how, but it would have taken you guys hours with that wood. Speaking of, is that even enough?" I asked.

Eli looked down at the fire, and Logan shook his head. Neither of them looked pleased with the amount of wood that had been gathered.

"I'll go out and look for more," Logan said.

Hopefully, he'd be able to find more wood we could use, but the storms had ripped out most of the trees and plants. Even where there might be something we could use, we wouldn't know it because it would be hidden by all the snow.

Thanks to the cold, long winter, nothing had a chance to grow back. The world around us was mostly empty. I didn't even know if anything would grow again if it ever did warm back up. Maybe the cold had already killed everything, and it would eventually get us too.

I sat down inside the little shelter on the opposite side Charlie picked. The fire crackled and popped as it grew, sufficiently warming the area.

Ryder adjusted the top of the shelter before sitting down next to me. "Not too shabby, huh?"

"Nope, not bad at all."

"It's actually quite awesome," Charlie said stretching her gloveless palms toward the fire. "You guys did a really amazing job."

Ryder grinned as he looked at every inch of the oval-shaped shelter. There were some holes the cold air seeped in through, but with the fire going, it was plenty warm. However, if there was a strong wind, the whole thing would probably blow down, but I kept that to myself.

I crossed my arms and leaned back using my backpack as a backrest. Ryder looked over his shoulder at me.

"Do you think we should stay here until morning?" he asked.

There was enough daylight left that we could travel a few more miles before nightfall, but my legs were killing me. They desperately needed a break.

"Well, you went to all the trouble to set this up, and the fire is quite nice. If everyone is good with stopping for the day, it's OK with me too," I said, and no one objected. I closed my eyes and tried not to think about the tightness in my muscles.

"How safe are we out here in the open like this?" Charlie asked, looking around. You could see for miles with the light from the sun, and there wasn't anything in sight. If anyone were approaching, they'd be easy to spot.

"Safe enough I think," Ryder said, rubbing his hands together.

I turned to Ryder. "How come you didn't see that guy coming?"

"What guy?" He squeezed his eyebrows together.

"When I first saw you. He attacked you."

"Oh! That guy," Ryder said wrapping his arm around his bent knee. "I saw him and ran. Trying to lead him away from Jacob's various hideouts. I tripped, fell, and he eventually caught up."

I glanced at Ryder's face where he'd been hit. It already looked as though it was healing.

"It wasn't the first time they caught me," Ryder said with a small laugh.

"You're lucky to be alive," Charlie said, as Logan leaned several pieces of wood against one another to form a pyramid over the fire.

Ryder looked down at his dirty fingernails with a sheepish grin on his face. It seemed as though he had liked the chase... the excitement. Although I was pretty sure he hadn't liked getting caught.

"Why put yourself at risk like that?" I asked looking at my own fingernails.

He shook his head. "I don't know. I guess it reminds me that I'm still alive."

"It's dumb that's what it is," Logan grunted as he sat down between Eli and Ryder.

"Bah," Ryder leaned forward and scanned the horizon. "You're all just jealous."

I drew in a slow breath. "I'm definitely not jealous."

"Yeah, that's because you're already out here. Danger is your middle name," Ryder said bumping me lightly with his elbow.

I loudly puffed out air between my lips. "That's not even close to accurate."

"Well, what's your story then?" Eli asked.

"I don't have a story," I said pressing my lips together tightly. Talking about what had happened was pretty much the last thing I wanted to do. These strangers didn't need to know about me, and I definitely wasn't about to tell them.

"Aw, come on," Eli said. "You know all about us, but we know nothing about you."

Ryder cleared his throat. It was a signal to his friends to stop asking me questions. He'd known what happened with my parents, and clearly he could tell it wasn't something I wanted to talk about.

It wasn't like they needed know. Knowing about my past wouldn't change anything.

———

They talked on and off until it was dark. Mostly they talked about things that were going on with Jacob and his army. The plans he'd made. His occasional mistakes.

Eli and Logan talked about how they were glad to be out of there. They liked it, but they knew they were fighting a losing battle. Charlie and Ryder didn't say much.

All I did was rub my calves every five minutes, listening to their various conversations. I was trying to massage away the stinging pins and needles sensation that hadn't stopped pecking at my legs since we quit walking.

"You're not used to a lot of traveling, are you?" Ryder whispered during a heated discussion between Eli and Logan about whether or not we'd actually find warmer weather.

I bit my cheek not wanting to admit the truth. He'd probably laugh at me. Then again, why should I even care if he did? He could just turn around and take his friends back to Jacob for all I cared.

"I'm not," I said wincing when I pushed down on a particularly sore spot.

"Here," Ryder grabbed my leg and pulled it onto his lap, "maybe I can help."

My eyes darted over to the others, but they were too engrossed in their conversation to even notice where my leg was. Charlie, who I would have assumed to have made a commotion if she'd noticed, appeared to be sleeping.

"How's that feel?" Ryder asked, his eyes glued to mine.

"Actually, it's helping." I couldn't help but sound surprised. I leaned back so I could rest my head on my backpack. It couldn't have taken longer than a minute for me to fall asleep.

When I opened my eyes again, it was morning. Ryder was still asleep next to me with his hand on my calf.

Logan was awake. He was busy kicking snow onto the fire that was already almost out. He glanced over at me and then out toward the southern horizon. "We should get moving."

I stretched my arms over my head and looked up at the clear sky. It was already much later than I would have liked.

"Yes, we should," I said, pushing myself up. My movements caused Ryder to wake, and seconds later Eli and Charlie stirred too.

"Ugh," Charlie groaned. "Sleeping outside is the absolute worst."

I pretended I hadn't heard her complaining as I picked up my backpack. My legs felt as good as new, thanks to Ryder. The others picked up their things, and we walked away.

I chewed on a bar of some kind that was probably long past its expiration date. It looked and tasted fine, so I couldn't really complain. The others gnawed on beef jerky and dried fruit from Jacob's storage. Their food looked absolutely mouthwatering compared to mine.

We'd only been walking for roughly an hour when I

saw the drops of blood in the snow. At first, there were just one or two drops, but then there were more. Bigger drops. Each one becoming closer and closer together.

I pointed at the ground, and Ryder nodded. His voice was just below a whisper. "Animal maybe?"

When the drops stopped abruptly so did we. My eyes scanned the ground, and I held out my arm to stop the others from continuing forward.

I spotted where the drops of blood continued, and I saw right where they came to an end.

Not far from us, someone was curled up into the fetal position. The man appeared to be breathing, but just barely. He was trying to hide behind a tree stump but failing. More than just the trail of blood gave him away.

Ryder stepped in front of me and stared at the lump. He spun around in a slow circle and scanned the area.

"I hope this isn't some kind of trap," he murmured.

"There isn't a single soul in sight," Eli said.

"You know as well as I do that doesn't mean anything," Ryder said, glancing at me as if he was hoping I'd share my opinion on how to proceed.

I bit my lip as I stared at the man on the ground. "There was a trail of blood, with only the one set of footprints as far as I could tell. He's definitely hurt."

"We could just keep going," Charlie said, and the man across the way help up his hand.

"Please," he shouted. I could tell he was summoning his last bits of strength to call out to us. "I'm injured. Can you help?"

He was hiding, but apparently not from us. My heartbeat slowed. Each beat stung my chest.

9

I nodded when Ryder glanced at me. He swallowed hard. Ryder had already guessed what I was going to do.

"Are you sure?" he asked.

"Do we have a choice?" I responded, my eyebrows squeezed together.

"We do," Logan grunted. "We can just keep going. Leave him."

If we left him, he'd probably die or be killed. I sucked in a deep breath and pulled out my gun. "Stay here if you want... or keep going."

Charlie groaned, and Logan threw his hands into the air as he turned away. I ignored them.

Each step I took towards the man lying on the bloodied snow was slow and careful. I wasn't exactly sure what the injured man would do to me, but it didn't matter.

I stayed back about ten feet and started walking in a semi-circle around the area, looking at him from every angle. He lifted up his bloody hand when he saw me looking at him.

"Please, not yet. I'm not ready to go," he said, his fingers trembling.

It didn't take more than a minute to realize it wasn't some kind of trick. The guy lying on the ground was quite hurt.

I tucked my gun back into my waistband and made my way over to him. The others were creeping closer, but far more apprehensively than I had. Charlie had her club up just above her shoulder ready to use it if need be.

I knelt down next to him and moved his scarf away from his mouth. "What happened to you?"

He twisted his head slightly, and I saw the tattoos on his neck. Shit. If the others saw them, they'd surely react. I held up my hand to stop them.

"I was attacked," he said between moans.

"I could have guessed that much. Where are you bleeding?"

He lifted his hand out of the snow. "There's a cut on my wrist. It won't stop bleeding."

I grabbed his arm and pulled back his sleeve. He cried out in pain.

"I think my arm is broken," he said through his clenched teeth.

"So, your arm, and the cut on your wrist... anything

else?" I asked staring at the blood crusted under his nose. He also had a cut just above his eyebrow, but I wasn't sure he'd even known it was there.

He hadn't shaved in days if not weeks. There was something in his sky-blue eyes that held me in my spot.

He shook his head. "I don't think you can help me. I'm going to die out here, aren't I?"

I leaned in close. "My friends over there... if they see your markings, you might have even less time than you think."

He stared at me for a moment. His eyebrows raised up slightly.

"Why don't you have any? The markings," he asked.

"Maybe you just don't see them," I said pushing myself to my feet. "Wait here."

He let out a gurgled chuckle. "Where else would I go?"

I jogged over to the others tucking my gloves into my jacket pockets. They all stared at me waiting for my report.

"He's hurt."

"No kidding?" Charlie said before I could finish.

I ignored her. "He seems to have a broken arm, a pretty significant laceration on his wrist, and various minor cuts and bruises."

"We're not set up to take care of anything like that," Logan said in his gruff voice.

"Let's just keep going," Charlie said.

I opened my backpack and took out the first aid kit

I'd packed. "The cuts can be bandaged, it's the arm I'm not sure what to do about."

"Stabilize it," Eli said rubbing his chin.

"How are we going to do that?" Charlie asked, looking at the guy on the ground out of the corner of her eye.

"I can help," Eli said grabbing my arm as I started walking back toward the guy.

Dammit.

He'd see the markings, but what choice did I have? I wasn't sure what to do about his arm, but Eli seemed confident.

"OK," I said, shifting my gaze toward Ryder. "You guys stay back. Guard the area."

Ryder cocked his head to the side. He pressed his lips together so hard the color vanished. He seemed suspicious.

The second Eli and I were out of earshot of the others, I took a deep breath. "He has markings on his neck."

Eli kept walking, but I could feel his eyes on me. Luckily, he hadn't changed anything about how he moved his arms or feet. "Then why exactly are we doing this?"

"I'm not really sure. He needs help. He said he was attacked. I can't just leave him lying in the snow. It's not like he can do anything to us in his condition."

Eli swallowed. "OK. As long as the others don't find

out. Charlie will use her club. And if she needs to, I won't stop her."

I nodded.

"We'll have to tell them eventually, right?" Eli asked.

"I think so… I just need more time to think."

The guy looked up at us, his eyes shifting back and forth between Eli and me. "Are you renegades?"

"I am," Eli answered quickly. "Is that going to be a problem?"

The guy on the ground shook his head.

"I'm not," I said, stiffening my jaw.

His eyes stayed focused on Eli. "I know what you think you see, but you have it all wrong."

"Do I? This is not the first time I've heard one of you say something along those lines," Eli said.

"Really, I promise you. I barely escaped them with my life. Look at me." The guy tried to move his arm, but it only jerked up slightly before he winced. "Please, please, please don't kill me. At least give me a chance to explain."

I knelt back down in the same spot I'd been in moments before. There was more blood pooled in the snow than when I had left.

"None of us are going to kill you," I said taking his hand gently so I could bandage the deep cut on his wrist first.

"Thank you, thank you," he said his voice almost fading away. "By any chance do you have any water to spare? The snow is just too cold."

I nodded. "Let me stop the bleeding first."

He focused his brilliant blue eyes on me and stared at me for a few moments before he spoke. "What's your name?"

My lips curled up on one side. "What's your name?"

"Shawn," he said without hesitation. "Now, you have to tell me yours."

"I have to, huh?" I asked.

He nodded weakly.

I drew in a long breath. "My name is Emery."

"And him?"

Eli groaned, watching me as I bandaged up his wrist. He crossed his arms, but then sighed before dropping down to his knees beside me.

"I'm Eli. Let me take a look at your arm."

Shawn tried to move his arm closer, but he was too weak. "I think it's broken."

"Do you think we can get it out of your jacket?" Eli asked.

"I'm not sure," Shawn said looking at his arm as if seeing it for the first time in a long time.

Eli pressed down on his arm through the jacket. "Let's try. The padding in your jacket is too thick."

I stepped around Shawn and held the arm of his jacket while they worked to wiggle his arm free. Shawn clenched his teeth, refusing to shout out his pain. He shivered the second his arm was out and the cool air brushed against his lightly clothed body.

Eli moved his hands up and down Shawn's arm. "I don't think it's broken."

"It fucking feels broken," Shawn said between his teeth. His anger was directed at the pain... at least I assumed it was.

"I believe you, but I think it's just a really nasty sprain. We should wrap it, and you'll need to keep it as still as you can. You'll be good as new in no time," Eli said, turning to me. "Do we have anything we can use?"

I chewed on my lip. "Oh, I have a spare shirt. Maybe we could rip that up and tie the strips together?"

"I'm not going to be good as new. I can barely move. I've lost so much blood." Shawn groaned as he shifted his weight slightly. "How did I even make it this far?"

I opened my backpack and took out my extra shirt, handing it to Eli. He glanced over his shoulder as he started tearing it into pieces.

"What are we going to tell them about Shawn and his tattoos?" Eli asked so quickly the words bumped into one another.

"Why?" My eyes followed his gaze.

"Because they're coming this way."

I pushed Shawn's scarf up, so it covered the markings on his neck.

"Just tell them the truth," Shawn said his eyes glassy. It almost looked as though he might lose consciousness.

"We don't know the truth," I said pasting a smile on my face.

"You do!" Shawn said with a grimace. "I'm Shawn, and I escaped from the hell I was living in. Isn't that enough?"

I shook my head. "I doubt it."

"Well, you better think of something fast," Eli said, tightening the strips together. "Hold him up."

I grabbed Shawn's shoulders and hoisted his heavy body up as best as I could. He might have been weak, but his actual body weight showed no signs of it.

Eli started wrapping his arm in a slightly bent position against his chest. The second he was finished, I pulled his jacket down and zipped it up.

"Thank you," Shawn said. "Are they going to kill me?"

"I hope not," I said refusing to let my smile waver. "We'll find out soon enough."

10

R yder and the others stood behind me. I didn't have to turn around to know their eyes were on Shawn.

His markings weren't visible, but I could feel the tension in the air. They were suspicious.

"This is Shawn," I said, as I finished bandaging the cut on his forehead. "He's in pretty rough shape."

No one said anything. The silence made my fingers shake.

Shawn looked into my eyes and then over my shoulder. His eyes moved from one person to the next.

Out of the corner of my eye, I saw Eli take a step back. He cleared his throat. "He's lost a lot of blood. There is a significant laceration on his wrist and a bad cut above his eye. I don't think his arm is broken, but it's a serious sprain."

"It's broken," Shawn muttered, but I don't think it had been loud enough for anyone to hear.

"I don't doubt for a second that it feels like it's broken," Eli said.

Apparently, it had been loud enough.

"OK," Ryder said. I could hear the snow crunching beneath his boots as he moved closer. "But how did he get the injuries?"

Just as I was about to blurt out that it was some kind of freak animal attack, Shawn held up a hand to stop me. He sucked in a deep breath.

"The Evolved attacked me when I tried to leave. They nearly killed me," Shawn said, placing his good hand over his scarf.

"That's an interesting choice of words," Logan said.

Shawn shook his head.

"You said 'leave' instead of something like, oh say, escape." Logan's eyes were glued to Shawn.

Shawn grinned slightly. "That's because I meant the word leave."

Logan bent his knees, crouching down like a wild beast ready to attack. Anger filled his eyes.

Charlie started swinging her club. She looked as though she was eager for someone to give her the go ahead.

Ryder held up his hands. "Let's all just stay calm. He can't even defend himself. We're not in any danger here."

"You sure about that?" Logan asked.

Ryder stood in front of Shawn and tapped the side of his torso with the tip of his boot. Shawn moaned as his eyes rolled back.

"Positive," Ryder said crouching down to look into Shawn's eyes. He studied him for a moment. "I think you have some explaining to do, huh?"

They stared at each other. It was almost like a contest to see who would look away first.

I was almost surprised when Shawn's eyes shifted downward. "Ask me whatever you want, but something tells me you aren't going to believe anything I have to say anyway."

"Why? Do you tell a lot of lies?" Ryder asked with a smirk.

"No. I have no reason to lie to you, but why would you believe someone you consider to be an enemy?" Shawn raised an eyebrow weakly.

"You're right. I probably won't."

Shawn sniffed. "Then I'm not sure why we should waste each other's time. After all it doesn't seem as though I have much left."

Ryder stood up and straightened the pack on his back. "We probably shouldn't." He took a step back. "We should really be on our way."

I narrowed my eyes at Ryder. If he noticed, he ignored me.

"About time," Charlie muttered.

Everyone stepped back behind Ryder. Everyone except for me.

"Will you be OK?" I asked.

Shawn released a breath he seemed to have been holding. "Yeah, sure. Don't worry about me. Thanks for the bandaging."

"No problem," I said, and walked over to the others. Shawn put his head down in the snow and closed his eyes.

It seemed like he was giving up.

There was no doubt in my mind that if we left, he would die. He wouldn't make it through the night.

Ryder sensed my hesitation. "Ready?"

"I don't think so," I said after a long pause.

"Oh, for Christ's sake," Charlie said hitting the snow with her club. Small white chunks flew up and heavily sprinkled back down making little holes in the undisturbed snow.

I turned my back to them. "Go ahead without me."

Ryder grabbed my arm before I'd made it more than two steps away. "You can't be serious?"

"Totally serious," I said jerking my arm away.

I walked toward Shawn. By the lack of sounds behind me, I knew they weren't following.

Shawn opened his eyes as I crouched down in front of him. He closed his eyes again without saying anything.

"First thing we're going to need to do is to get you on your feet," I said setting down my backpack.

"Leave me. Go on with your friends."

I didn't turn to see how far they'd gone. They'd be

fine without me. It wasn't like I had even wanted them with me in the first place.

"Don't be so dramatic," I said stepping over him and slipping my arms under his. "If I leave you here, the wolves will get you."

"Let them."

"And waste the bandages? No way. I'll do whatever I must to keep those bandages safe."

Shawn shook his head. "Now who's being dramatic? I saw your handy box of bandages. You'll be fine without the ones you've given me."

"Did you see your wrist? I used nearly half my gauze. Come on, use your legs, I didn't see anything wrong with those," I said pulling upward carefully using as much of my strength as I could muster.

"You didn't see them because my pants are on," Shawn mumbled. He grunted and pushed upward with his good arm.

He got to his feet and tried to stand up straight, but the pain wouldn't allow it. I walked around to the front of him and picked up my pack. His eyelids were heavy.

"I don't know why you didn't just tell them why you left The Evolved," I said with a sigh.

"They wouldn't have believed me. When the renegades find The Evolved, they kill them. No questions asked. I'm lucky to be alive."

"We're all lucky to be alive don't you think?"

Shawn shrugged his good shoulder. "I suppose so,

but luck only lasts so long, and if you stay with me, you'll probably be cutting your luck short."

"For what it's worth, I don't think they would have killed you. They didn't kill me." I finally looked up and saw they'd made a fair amount of progress.

"Why would they kill you?"

I shrugged.

"Are you dangerous?"

"Maybe," I said grinning as I looked down at the snow.

"If you want to go with them, I'm sure you can still catch up."

I shook my head. "Don't give it a second thought. Come on, let's walk." He moved slowly, but he was moving. "So, what was it like with The Evolved? Are you as evil as they say?"

"They said I was evil?"

"No, I guess not. It was more like you guys, The Evolved, want to rule the world and you'll take out anyone that stands in your way."

Shawn laughed. "I'm not sure they have that part wrong. But it's not true about me."

"So, you're like them? A renegade?"

"I wish," Shawn said glancing at me.

The area around his eyes was dirty and speckled with crusted on blood, but his eyes were so pure and captivating. When he looked into my eyes, it was like he could see everything I was seeing... feel everything I was feeling. It was almost too intimate.

"What they call me is far worse than being a renegade. I'm a traitor," Shawn said.

"That's worse than a renegade?"

Shawn bobbed his head up and down slowly. "Much."

"Were you a traitor?"

A big smile appeared on his face. "Not really, but I guess, in a way, maybe I was because I was thinking about it. I was thinking about doing something to sabotage their whole operation."

"Had you been with them long?"

"All my life."

"Then why the change of heart?"

Shawn glanced at me. My heart skipped a beat when he looked into my eyes.

"They did something I couldn't be OK with. I couldn't look the other way," Shawn said.

"Dare I ask?"

Shawn's lips formed a perfectly straight line. "There was a young girl. Maybe fourteen."

"Do I want to know?"

"Probably not. The man leading our particular base was a tyrant. He'd slit someone's throat for questioning him. Or break fingers just to prove a point. I'd seen him do those things on more than one occasion," Shawn held up his hand with two crooked fingers. "Anyway, he wanted a wife."

I swallowed hard. "The girl?"

Shawn nodded. "But it didn't stop with her. He

wanted another. She was ten. I can close my eyes and still hear her mother's painful cries as they pulled her daughter away from her."

"That's terrible."

"Her mother was found hanging from a tree less than twenty-four hours later."

My stomach turned. "Were things always like that?"

"I grew up on a different base, when I turned twenty they transferred me. It wasn't bad at first, but things just kept getting worse and worse. I should have done something to help those girls."

"You would have been killed," I said softly.

"No kidding. I was almost killed, and I hadn't done anything." Shawn stumbled but held out his hand to indicate that he was fine.

"So, why did they come after you if you hadn't actually done anything?"

"I'd made the mistake of telling someone I thought I could trust what I thought about Chet starting his harem of young girls."

We walked in silence for several minutes. By the look on his face, it appeared as though he was reliving the whole experience.

"So, yeah, here I am. In the middle of nowhere, not sure if I'll make it through the night." He looked down at his dragging feet. "I'm not cut out for this. I had it easy at the base."

"You'll be fine. All you need is some rest and something to eat. How long have you been out here wandering around?" I asked looking him up and down.

Shawn shook his head. "I'm not sure. A week give or take."

"You really must have lost a lot of blood."

He nodded. "I believe I did. Thanks again for the bandages. You probably saved my life."

"Don't mention it." I smiled.

"OK." He smiled back. "Hey, look, your friends stopped. They've probably decided to kill me after all."

My hand jerked toward my hip. I was overreacting. They weren't going to do anything although Charlie seemed to be itching to use her club.

But why had they stopped? I guess Shawn and I would find out soon enough.

11

Ryder stood in front of the others protectively. Charlie had her club resting on her shoulder, her head cocked to the side as she sneered at us unnecessarily. Or maybe that was just her usual expression.

"Something wrong?" I said as we approached.

"No, except the big dummy here doesn't want to leave you behind," Charlie said flicking her eyes up toward the sky.

I looked at Ryder, but his eyes were on Shawn. Why did he care so much about what happened to me? It wasn't like we'd even known each other for that long. Sure, I didn't want anything to happen to him either, but I didn't want anything to happen to any of us. Not even Charlie.

"We should probably kill you," Ryder said eying Shawn.

"If you're going to do it, just get it over with," Shawn said throwing his good hand in the air. "Really though, I think if you were you going to, you probably would have done so by now."

My dad was probably turning in his grave. I was breaking his rules, but hey, at least I was still alive. That had to count for something, didn't it?

"No one is killing anyone," I said, holding up my palm. "Instead, why don't you listen to what he has to say. Or you guys can go your way, and we can go ours."

"They are all liars," Logan said, turning his head and spitting on the ground near his feet. "Can't trust a word they say."

I shook my head. "I don't think he's lying."

"OK, Shawn," he said, moving his mouth as though his name had tasted like mud, "what do you have to say? What is going to change our minds about you?" The cocky grin on his face even annoyed me.

Shawn groaned and looked at me for several seconds before he turned to them and told them the same story he'd told me. They all watched him as if they were trying to find something wrong with what he was saying. Something that would prove that they were right and that he was, in fact, a bad guy.

Instead, Shawn got a little choked up when he talked about leaving the girls behind with that creep that was in charge. If it was an act, he was very good. He'd even gone so far as to almost die to pull it all off.

"If it wasn't for Emery, I don't think I would have made it through the night lying in the snow, now I actually have a chance," Shawn said.

"She's foolish," Charlie muttered.

"Is she though?" The way Shawn looked at her made her shift her weight back and forth. "Maybe what this world needs is more people like her. More people that won't steal, hurt, or kill others for whatever their cause. People that help one another, but what do I know?"

Logan chuckled. "Kill or be killed. That is unfortunately the reality of our situation. This is the world we live in."

"It doesn't have to be," Shawn said, blowing out a puff of air as he shook his head. He liked the sound of his words, as did I, but it was like he realized just how ridiculous it all sounded.

"Nobody is killing anyone. I mean, really, he can barely walk," I said staring at his empty sleeve. "He's with me, and if anyone has a problem with it, they're free to go. I'm not keeping anyone here. You all wanted to come with me for whatever crazy reason."

Ryder crossed his arms. "What if you're making a mistake?"

"I guess it's a risk I'm willing to take. You guys are all here with me, for all I know that was a mistake." I adjusted my gloves as the cold air prickled my wrists. "It's not like I have any part in this war. He's just as much of a risk to me, as all of you are. At least that's how I see it."

"Then you see it wrong," Logan said. "They are trying to wipe us all out. They wouldn't hesitate to slit your throat, or maybe even worse."

"Worse?" I asked.

Logan bobbed his head. "Didn't you hear his story? Lots of stuff like that goes on with The Evolved. That's probably not even the worst of it. If they took you in as a slave, you'd beg them to kill you. Isn't that right?"

Shawn looked at me and nodded. He seemed to drift away as his eyes filled with sadness.

"Well then, maybe we should keep moving," I said taking a step forward.

Ryder looked at me and then back at Shawn. "If he tries anything even the slightest bit suspicious, I'll do what I have to. Is that understood?"

I wanted to tell Ryder he didn't make the rules for me, but before I could even open my mouth, Shawn agreed to his terms. He held out his hand, and Ryder apprehensively shook it.

As we walked, I took out my water bottle and offered Shawn a drink. He took a small sip at first, but then something took over, and he swallowed down a big gulp.

"Sorry," he said passing it back. He wiped his lower lip with the back of his hand. "Thirsty, I guess."

"Do you have gloves?" I asked looking at his red fingers.

He shook his head. "Where are we going? I don't know of anywhere that's safe, do you?"

My mind flooded with random warnings from my dad. One of them being to never tell where I was headed. I'd broken so many rules, but I decided to keep this one, at least for now.

I shook my head and chewed on my cheek. It was already raw from having gnawed on it far too much recently.

"Either way, I'm grateful for everything you've done for me." Shawn bowed his head slightly.

"Anyone would have done the same," I said, and Charlie huffed loudly.

"No, they wouldn't," Shawn said smiling. But it was an odd sight... his perfect white toothy grin, and his dirty, blood-splattered face made an interesting combo.

I shrugged. "I'm not those people I guess. Besides, I asked you not to mention it."

"That was the last time. I promise," he said flashing me his perfect grin again.

Ryder was quiet while we walked. In fact, his whole group was. It was as if they were waiting for something to happen. For something to go wrong. I could feel just how on edge they all were, but what was weird was that I didn't feel it. Maybe that should have worried me, but it hadn't.

"Holy balls, look at that," Eli said slapping his gloved hand against his thigh.

With Shawn in his condition, I don't think we could have been any luckier. It was some kind of miracle, or maybe it was just a mirage.

The others ran ahead while I helped Shawn along. I couldn't help but smile as I watched them run.

12

There, in the middle of the woods was an old brick house. Somehow it had managed to survive the big storm, the war, and whatever else had gone on while I was hiding out with my family.

Ryder turned around and smiled at me. "No footprints, but we still have to check it out."

He pulled out a knife, and Charlie held her club up as they entered the unlocked front door.

"It's in pretty good condition," Shawn said looking the house over as we approached.

Eli and Logan walked around the perimeter, one went left and the other to the right. Their eyes alternated from the horizon down to the ground. When they met up at the front of the house, they entered.

"No screams or sounds of that club bashing in heads," Shawn said. "That's promising."

"I don't even want to know what that would sound

like," I said with a disgusted grimace.

"Hopefully, you won't have to."

I looked up at Shawn my eyebrow raised. "Would we even be able to hear that out here?"

"The screams? Definitely."

"Ha," I said helping him as we made our way to the house. I looked him up and down. "You seem to be doing a bit better already."

Shawn glanced at his wrist. "I think stopping, or maybe just slowing the bleeding helped a lot. Trust me though, this isn't easy. I'm fighting every urge to just lay down and give up."

Before we even made it to the porch, Ryder popped his head out of the front door. "All clear. It's a disaster in there though."

"It's a roof over our heads, what more could we ask for?" Shawn said, walking past Ryder as he hobbled his way inside.

I tried to follow Shawn, but Ryder took a step forward and held out his arm to stop me. "Can we talk a minute?"

"Yeah, of course. What's up?" I asked taking off my backpack and setting it near my feet, so I could feel it resting against my leg. I looked up at him and crossed my arms.

"Are we OK?" he asked, shifting his weight nervously.

I squinted at him. "Yeah, why wouldn't we be?"

"Several reasons, but I guess mainly because I didn't

want Shawn to come with us. I feel bad about walking away from you, but I don't trust him. I still don't," he said looking down at his feet.

"Just because Shawn was stuck living with the bad guys, doesn't mean he is a bad guy."

Ryder cocked his head to the side. "It doesn't mean he's a good guy either."

"I understand that of course, but I gave you guys a chance, why not him too?"

"You gave us a chance because we saved you from those creeps and I brought you back to Jacob."

I nodded. "True, but I could have just walked away. You would have let me go."

"Oh, is that right? I would have, huh?"

I was absolutely right. He would have. There was no doubt in my mind.

I looked over his shoulder trying to see inside the house, but all I could see was darkness and shadows. "I don't know what it is, but something tells me he's telling the truth."

"What if they're out there right now looking for him? Maybe they want to finish him off."

"Then we better get him as far away as fast as we can, right?"

Ryder stared at the horizon. I turned, so we were shoulder to shoulder. I could see for miles. There wasn't anything out there except for a few broken trees and snow covering the ground for as far as the eye could see.

We were living in a desolate world, and while we haven't traveled far, nothing about the landscape had changed. Everything looked the same since I'd left my home. For all I knew, for all any of us knew, it would continue on like this until we couldn't walk anymore. Until the brutal winter took us all out for good.

"This house seems pretty decent," Ryder said. "Maybe we should just stay here for a while."

"We aren't even all that far from Jacob, not to mention the fact that I don't think Shawn had traveled all that far after he escaped. He was in pretty rough shape. The Evolved could be closer than we think. Maybe even closer than Jacob realizes." I took off my gloves and shoved them into my pockets. "We can stay for a day or two, or however long it takes for Shawn to heal up a bit more, but any longer is too risky."

Ryder groaned. "Ugh, you're probably right. I just hate being out in the open because then I worry about you, and the others too."

"I'll be fine," I said raising my eyebrow, "and so will the others. Don't forget about yourself while you're so busy worrying about everyone else."

Ryder laughed. "The one thing I don't do. Never have worried about myself."

"Let's go inside," I said as a cool breeze drifted past, stinging my cheeks.

Before I turned toward the house, an icy shiver ran up and down my spine. I quickly scanned the horizon unable to shake the feeling that someone was watching Ryder and me on that porch.

Once we were inside, Ryder locked the door and closed the curtains. Eli and Logan were working to push all of the debris and other random junk to one side of the room.

There was a fireplace, but of course, there wasn't any wood.

The floors were covered with so much dirt and grime that you could see every footprint that had been made since we'd gotten there. There weren't any pictures or art hanging on the walls. The house was mostly bare. Anything that would have been of any use to us had been stripped out long ago.

The place didn't feel like a home, it felt like a shell... a cocoon, but at least for the most part, it was warm and hopefully, it would do its job keeping us safe through the night.

Charlie found a broken broom that only had half of its thick straw-like bristles remaining. She swept the floors as best as she could, trying to remove the build-up of dirt.

Shawn hadn't cared at all about the filthy floor. He was already lying down, groaning as he held his bad arm steady with his good arm.

I started looking through the rooms and closets, hoping I could find something to put down on the floor. The snow outside was cold, but at least it was clean.

I was inside what had once upon a time been a bedroom. The metal-framed bed was still there, but everything else had been ripped out. The closets were empty and based on the accumulation of dust and dirt on the plastic shelving unit, they'd been raided a long time ago.

"Oh!" I said noticing the blanket that was on the bed just as I was about to leave the room. I reached out and grabbed the corner, yanking it hard toward me.

When I saw the skeleton practically fused to the bed, I couldn't stop the squeaking gasp that escaped from between my lips. The noise was so loud and odd, they must have heard it in the next room.

"Oh, Jesus," Ryder said as he stepped up next to me. He turned his head away and scrunched up his nose.

I dropped the corner of the blanket as though it was contaminated with some kind of infectious disease. My stomach turned. Only seconds ago, it had been unnecessarily keeping the dead body warm.

The smell from the corpse stung my nostrils. I don't know how I hadn't noticed it when I first came into the room. Perhaps it had settled and only filled the room after I'd moved the blanket.

My stomach twisted harder, and all I could think about was getting out of the room. I covered my mouth and pushed my way past Ryder.

Seconds later, I heard Ryder closing the door. "This room is off limits."

"Claiming it for yourself?" Charlie asked with a silly giggle.

"No, it's already been claimed." Ryder stared at her as if trying to send her a telepathic message.

"Oh?" Charlie raised an eyebrow clearly not receiving his message.

Ryder stomped over to the fireplace. "Yeah, and he, or she, is still in there. Trust me when I say you don't want to go in there. That's not something you can unsee."

"We've seen some shit," Charlie said crossing her arms. She looked as though she was offended by his words.

"Just trust me OK?" Ryder said looking up at her. "Let it go."

He stood and walked over to Logan, who was going through the piles of junk to see what he could use for the fireplace.

"Let's go get some wood," Ryder said.

Eli stepped out of the kitchen breathing heavily. "No need," he said, and they both turned to him. "I think there's some stuff we can use downstairs."

Eli, Logan, Ryder, and Charlie all left the room to go have a look at whatever Eli had found. The room was quiet, and it felt like it was the first time I'd breathed since I'd met them.

I sat down on the somewhat cleaner floor next to Shawn. His body slowly moved up and down with each breath.

I looked over to see if his eyes were closed. It didn't surprise me to see that they were. I could see them jerking around under his eyelids while he dreamed.

Shawn didn't seem to care even a little that he was stuck with people he would have once considered his enemies. The thought of what they might do to him wasn't keeping him awake with worry. But maybe falling asleep had been out of his control considering his condition. Maybe he had fought it but lost the battle.

Shawn needed the rest. He needed to get better.

The sooner he was well, the quicker we could leave this place behind, maybe find something similar far, far away from everyone up here in the north. We just had to keep going.

South.

It would be warmer.

I could grow food. Things had to be better. All we had to do was get there.

There would be fresh fish and plenty of water. I could have that life again, and I wouldn't be alone.

Sure Charlie would be there, but maybe that was better than being stuck alone for the rest of my time on this planet. I would at least tell myself that it would be.

The gang ran up the stairs and had a fire going in minutes. The area in front of the fire warmed up rather quickly, and I was able to take off all my winter gear. I laid down and stared at the flames.

"Warm beans tonight, boys," Eli said digging in his backpack.

"And girls," Charlie said, sitting cross-legged in front of the fire.

Ryder looked out the window and sighed loudly. "It's not going to last. We're going to need to find more."

"I've seen several wolves over the last few days," Shawn said. "Could try to trap one. Or use that club if you can get close enough."

Charlie grinned as if it was some kind of compliment to her.

"Probably won't get close enough. But you might be on to something. Perhaps we can construct a trap with the junk in the basement."

After we ate, Logan stared out the window into the darkness while Ryder and Eli worked downstairs. Occasionally, I'd hear something banging or falling. I wasn't exactly sure what the noise was, but hopefully, it was the sounds of progress.

My stomach rumbled, and I closed my eyes. Visions of the feasts I used to eat with my mom and dad filled my mind.

It felt so real when my dad leaned closer and whispered into my ear. I could still hear his words when my eyes popped open.

Leave.

Run.

Don't trust them.

13

When I woke, there was a bit of light coming in through the windows. It wasn't morning, but it would be soon.

I was alone near the dwindling flames. After blinking several times, I spotted them all looking out of the front windows.

Shawn and Eli were at one window and Logan, Ryder and Charlie were squeezed together at the other. I couldn't even guess as to what was going on.

"What are you all doing?" I said walking up behind Shawn and Eli. I tried to peek between their shoulders, but I couldn't see anything.

"Shh!" Eli said over his shoulder.

I lowered my voice quieter than a whisper. "OK, what's going on?"

"Wolf," Shawn said.

"You're kidding," I said pushing my way between them.

I could feel Eli's eyes on me, but I ignored them. It wasn't like I was going to scare it away from inside the house.

"Maybe we should use her gun," Charlie whispered.

I was already shaking my head before anyone could even ask.

"Might be too loud. Plus is anyone here a good shot?" Ryder asked.

"I am, but we're not using my gun," I said touching the cool metal to make sure it was still there.

The wolf paused. Its ears twitched as if sensed someone was watching it. Then, it bolted.

"Nooooo!" Charlie whined as she stomped over to the fire.

I walked over to Ryder who was still at the window. He was probably hoping it would come back.

"How's the trap coming along?" I asked.

He looked into my eyes and smiled. "It's never going to work. It's a sad contraption made from random metal bars. Wolf kicks over one of the bars, and a bigger bar falls on its head."

"Sounds like it could work."

"The trap is smaller than that wolf was. Maybe we could catch a fox," Ryder said, crossing his arms.

"So you're not even going to try?" I asked, my eyebrows squeezed together.

Ryder shook his head. "Nah, of course we'll try, but my expectations are low. Yours should be too."

"It probably won't even come back," Eli said stepping up between us. "Let's go set it up in case he does come back."

"Go on ahead, I'll be right down," Ryder said, turning back toward me. "Want to come with?"

I could feel the cold air blowing in through the cracks in the window frame. I bit my lip and shook my head. "Think I'll watch from the window."

"OK, but you'll miss out on all the fun," Ryder said glancing over at Shawn as he picked up his jacket.

"I'm all about taking those risks," I said as he walked away. He looked at me over his shoulder, his expression was so contorted I couldn't decipher it.

Logan followed them downstairs. It was so quiet, I could hear their muffled voices through the floorboards.

"He likes you, you know?" Charlie said, her expression blank as she twisted her fingers. "Not just like, normal like. A bigger like."

I don't know why but I quickly glanced at Shawn. His eyes were closed, and his breathing was slow.

"Not him." Charlie shifted her eyes downward. "Ryder."

My mouth felt dry. I moved my head side to side as if I was trying to shake her words away from my ears.

"It's true," she said, hugging her knees to her chest.

"Did he say that?" I asked, my voice felt as though it was getting stuck in my throat.

Her shoulders bobbed. "He didn't need to."

"Listen, I think you have it all wrong."

"No, you listen," Charlie said leaning forward, her eyes wide. "I've known him my whole life. Trust me. I know."

I chewed on my lip. "Well, even if it were true, I'm not sure what you want me to do about it. I just want to get... where I'm going without trouble."

Charlie cracked her neck to one side and then the other. Her eyes quickly shifted to Shawn and then back at me.

"Nothing. I just thought you should know," she said resting her head back against the dirty wall. "Maybe we should melt some snow, wash our hair in the sink."

At first I thought she was joking, but as it turned out, she was just crazy. Charlie was absolutely serious.

"Did you see the sink?" I asked. "It's covered in filth."

"Clean it." Charlie shrugged.

"Pass."

She tossed her long pigtails back. "Suit yourself stink-head."

"Oh, Christ," I muttered, and she flounced out of the room.

Something in the basement crashed loudly and rang out for several seconds. Metal. What the hell were they doing down there?

Shawn shifted his weight and groaned, keeping his eyes closed. He cleared his throat. "I wanted to say something, but I thought it might be rude."

"What's that?" I asked.

"It's about your stinky head," Shawn said unable to keep the smile off his face.

I lightly kicked my foot against his thigh, and he winced. "Oh shit, sorry," I said getting closer. "I thought it was your other side. Dammit. I wasn't thinking, are you OK?"

"I'm fine. It's fine, stink—"

"Don't say it. Don't even think it," I said pressing my fingers to his lips. The second I heard them coming up the stairs I pulled back. My cheeks felt warm... perhaps I was too close to the barely burning fire.

Shawn's eyes were on me. His lip curled up at the ends into a curious smile. If only I could read minds.

"All right, we're going to go set this up," Ryder announced as they banged pieces of their trap against the wall and then against the door as they exited.

The door closed and Shawn lightly touched my knee. My heart felt as though it skipped a beat when I looked into his sparkling eyes. I could stare at them forever.

"The Sink is clean!" Charlie said bouncing into the room. I inched back and turned to look at her. "And I found a bucket to collect my snow."

"It's cracked," I said.

"If you have a better bucket let me know," she said

as she opened the door and disappeared from the house.

I could feel Shawn's eyes on me.

"It's quiet," Shawn whispered.

"Yeah, maybe too quiet," I said pushing myself to my feet. I walked over to the window just so that I could breathe normally again.

The guys were taking turns trying to get a section of their trap to balance just right. They'd get it up, and in seconds it would tumble back down to the ground.

I smiled when Ryder kicked the snow in frustration. My dad had taught me how to trap animals but never anything as big as a wolf. More like something that would feed just one person.

Shawn groaned, and the floorboards creaked underneath him as he tried to get up.

"Do you need something?" I asked.

"Yeah, to get up." The irritation in his voice was unmistakable. "Sorry," he said turning to me, "I'm not used to lying around all day."

"It's probably good for you to move around."

Shawn walked over to the window and peered out at them. He smiled. "That's never going to work."

"It's worth a shot," I said with a small shrug.

"Sure. Yeah." He turned to me and his eyes caught mine. "Do you think what Charlie said is true?"

I shook my head. "What did Charlie say?"

"About Ryder liking you." He winced as he touched the cut near his eye. Shawn looked at his fingers, I could tell he expected to see them covered in blood. A tiny, perfectly round circle of blood had seeped through the bandage, but nothing at all major.

"I doubt it. She doesn't like me. She's probably just screwing with me."

Shawn shook his head. "I don't know. I think she's telling the truth."

"Why do you say that?" I asked looking away from his perfect eyes.

"I don't know. Does she have a reason to lie about it?"

"No, but she's just guessing."

He shrugged. "An educated guess perhaps."

"I don't know, why are we even talking about this?" I asked as he took a step closer. My heart pounded a hard beat. What was happening? Why did I have to react to him in such a way? Was I afraid of him because of all of their talk about The Evolved?

Shawn stepped in front of me and looked into my eyes. "We can talk about whatever you want. I'd like to thank you again for saving me, but I know if I brought it up, it would just piss you off."

"You got that right," I said with wide eyes. "Let's talk about something that has nothing to do with me."

"That's too bad. I find you very interesting," Shawn said leaning forward ever so slightly. He was gazing deeply into my eyes as if he was trying to find something... something that would reveal everything about me to him.

We were inches apart when the front door swung open. I abruptly stepped away from Shawn as if I had been caught doing something I shouldn't have been.

The second they were all inside Ryder slammed the door shut. They were all breathing heavily.

"What's going on?" I asked.

Ryder's palms were pressed against the door. He looked over his shoulder at Shawn and me.

"They're out there," Ryder said.

"Who's out there?" I asked.

I'd seen Ryder fighting with one of The Evolved, but he hadn't looked anywhere near as frightened as he was now. "It's the Natives."

1 4

I ran over to the window and scanned the horizon. There wasn't anything out there, at least as far as I could tell, that would have caused such a fright, but they were spooked to the core.

"Make sure all the doors and windows are locked," Ryder said as he moved around checking the various doors and windows in the room. He stopped and glared at the others. "What are you waiting for? Help me!"

Everyone started to move around. Even Shawn was trying to help although at a much slower pace due to his injuries. A switch had been flipped, and they all seemed to be in fight, or rather defense, mode. Except for me. I couldn't quite understand what was so bad about the natives. In fact, based on their definition, I would have been considered a native.

"What will they do if they find us?" I asked.

"This group is nasty. We've seen their work before," Logan said in a rough, almost angry voice. "They'll kill us."

"And then they'll eat us. That order if we're lucky," Charlie said running back to the front window, moving the curtain ever so slightly out of the way so she could peek out.

It seemed strange to me that both of these groups, Shawn from The Evolved and the others, ex-renegades or whatever, were both equally afraid of the natives.

It wasn't like their groups hadn't killed others. But I guessed the difference was the part about the natives going so far as to fill their bellies with their enemies.

"Your groups have killed for survival too, why is what they are doing any more terrifying?" I asked as I stared out the window, still not seeing what they had seen.

"We're doing it because we are fighting for what we believe in. We take no pleasure in it. I don't even know why they're doing it," Eli said.

Logan grunted. "Because they can."

"Maybe, or maybe they're doing it for what they believe in. Couldn't that be the case for them?" I asked.

Ryder grabbed my shoulders and looked into my eyes. His eyebrows were pinched together. "It doesn't matter why. They'll kill you if they find us here. For all I know, they already saw us. I think we got inside quick enough, but if not, there are a good twenty of them out there. They won't hesitate to kill us, all of us, and that includes you."

"But I'm not a renegade or one of The Evolved," I said shaking my head. Surely, they'd see I wasn't marked.

"It doesn't matter. They don't give a shit about any of that. They'd kill a native if they wanted to," Ryder said.

I could feel just how tense the situation was making him by how tightly he was gripping my shoulders. "I understand but you live with the threat of dying every single day, I don't understand what makes the natives so much worse."

"They like to play with their food," Logan said, opening the bedroom door we weren't supposed to open.

The putrid odor filled the room and stung my nostrils. Thankfully he was in and out of the room in seconds.

"Remember those three guys that tied you up?" Ryder asked. "They were natives, but it was a new way of life for them. What they did was nothing compared to what seasoned natives will do to us."

"They'll take over this whole place. Torture us. Store us in the basement, killing us one by one, and they'll do it with a bloody smile on their faces. They don't have a specific place they call home. They'll stay here as long as they have food," Charlie said, frowning. "I don't want to see that happen to any of us."

Her eyes quickly shifted to Ryder and stayed glued to him. It didn't seem as though she was scared of the natives only for herself.

I instantly realized why Charlie hadn't liked me. It was because she had some kind of feelings for Ryder. As far as she was concerned, I had gotten in her way.

"What about the fire? Won't they see the smoke rising out of the chimney?" I asked.

"Jesus Christ," Shawn said, quickly hobbling over to the fireplace. He moved so slowly that Ryder beat him to the already low flames.

Ryder held out his hand. "Charlie, give me your bucket of snow."

She didn't argue. Charlie handed it over, and Ryder tossed it on what remained of the fire. The flames almost instantly died out, but there was still smoke wafting out of the sizzling wood. Surely the natives would see it.

"Dammit!" Ryder said throwing the bucket against the wall.

"There's nothing we can do about it," Eli said taking quick breaths as if he was about to hyperventilate. He quickly moved over to the window. His head slowly turned toward us, and he swallowed hard. "They're closer. They're coming."

"How much longer do you think we have?" Ryder asked as he looked at our things scattered all over the floor.

Eli shook his head. "Five minutes, maybe ten at best. Not enough time."

"What if we sneak out the back?" I asked turning toward the back door.

Ryder's eyes settled on Shawn for a split-second. "We won't get far with him. They'll catch up to us. Our chances are probably better if we stay here. I'm not sure how safe we'd be in the open against their arrows."

"Arrows?" I asked.

Ryder nodded.

"Are you sure? Out there we can run, but in here we are sitting ducks," I said rubbing my thumb against my lower lip.

"I can't run," Shawn said. "You guys should go. Leave while you still can."

I shook my head. "I'm not leaving anyone behind."

"I'll hide downstairs. It's the best chance you guys have."

"We can all hide downstairs. Maybe they won't even come here." I crossed my arms as I walked over to the window. I shivered. Without the fire, the room was quickly getting cold. "Sure, they'll see the smoke, but they don't know what's waiting inside the house. Maybe they'll think they are the ones in danger."

I had my gun, and while I didn't have twenty bullets, maybe I'd only need to use one. All I had to do was scare them enough so that they'd leave.

I pulled the gun out of my waistband and looked out the window. They were out there. I could finally see them, but they were still far enough away that we could try to run.

"Maybe that could work." Ryder's head was bobbing up and down slowly, while he stared at my gun. "Maybe."

"One gun won't scare them," Logan said.

"They don't know how many we have," I said with a shrug.

Ryder shook his head. "There's no way to know for sure what will happen, but it might just be the best chance we have to survive this. They aren't going to want to lose their men and women. One could be all we need."

"But we can't actually use the gun," Eli said.

"Why not?" I asked. It wasn't like I was just dying to use it, but if I had to, there wasn't anything that was going to stop me from firing at them.

"If you shoot, and kill one of them, they'll charge. How many can you kill before they get to the house?" Ryder asked.

I shrugged. Probably not all of them, but the house was locked. Even if a few of them managed to get inside, we'd be able to overpower them.

"I don't have enough bullets, but it'll take them a while to get inside. I think we'd have the upper-hand," I said looking at Ryder. "You have your knife and Charlie has her club."

I wished I had more bullets or even more guns, but I didn't. Even though my dad had stockpiled bullets, over the years, we'd used them over time. It was something we couldn't ever have enough of. At one point he'd stopped bringing them back. It was like they had become extinct.

I had what was left, and it wasn't even close to being enough. But if I had to use them, I would.

"They're coming this way," Charlie said, backing away from the window. She moved all the way back to the fireplace and hugged herself.

We didn't have any options. We were going to stand our ground.

I watched the group of natives as they approached. Their gang was mostly men, but there were several women with them huddled together at the back of the group.

They alternated between looking at the ground and up at the house. If the smoke that wisped out of the chimney hadn't given us away, surely, they'd seen our footprints in the snow. For all I knew, maybe they could even guess as to how many people were inside the house based on the tracks in the snow.

One of the guys pointed at the trap, and a few of them laughed. The others wore unreadable expressions.

They were hairy, dirty and dressed similarly. The three men in front all had hoods made from furry animal heads. Two of which seemed to be wolves and the one leading them wore a bear.

Everyone in the group wore cloaks made from various animal hides and fur. They looked warm and not at all desperate.

There wasn't a single one of them that looked the way we did. They weren't thin, nor did they have dark circles under their eyes from lack of a good night's sleep. All of them appeared to be quite healthy.

Some of the women toward the back of the group had round bellies. If I had to guess, I'd say it wouldn't be long before they were carrying little fur-covered bundles.

"OK away from the windows," Ryder said putting his hands on my shoulders and pulling me back gently. "Everyone."

We all stepped away, forming a straight line. Our shoulders touching as we kept our eyes glued to the front windows, breathing heavily even though we couldn't see them anymore.

Ryder paced back and forth, taking each step slowly and carefully as if he were walking on thin ice. He stopped every third pass to peek out the window. He'd pause for a moment before stepping back to pace again. His fingers trembled slightly as he ran them through his hair.

"What's going on out there?" Logan whispered.

"Nothing." Ryder pinched his chin. "They're just standing there... staring at the house."

I imagined them huddled together debating about

what they should do. I hoped they were just as worried about us as we were about them.

Each breath I took was shaky. Every inhale squeezed my lungs causing mild discomfort that tensed my shoulder muscles. It was like I was afraid they might hear my breathing.

"Maybe they'll leave," I said after my exhale.

"Maybe," Ryder said pacing back and forth his usual three times. He stopped and looked out the window again. "But they haven't yet."

My heart started to pound so hard it felt like my entire body was shaking. Shawn was to my right, and I was pretty sure he could feel my body jerking with each rapid beat where our shoulders touched.

I jumped when I felt a hand lightly touch my back. Shawn's warm hand wrapped around mine.

He leaned close, his eyes filled with concern. "It'll be OK," Shawn whispered, as he moved his thumb up and down on the back of my hand. "I won't let anything happen to you."

I couldn't say anything. I couldn't even move. All I could do was stare into his eyes.

"I owe you one," he said with a nervous chuckle.

Ryder was staring out the window longer than he had the other times. His eyes were focused on some kind of movement. There was something going on out there, but I couldn't see what it was.

Logan must have realized it too. "What's going on now?"

"They're looking at something, but I can't see what it is," Ryder said, his hands clenched together into tight fists.

I couldn't stop my feet. Before I knew it, I was standing in front of the other window. Ryder hadn't seemed to notice I'd moved, and the others hadn't stopped me.

One of the natives raised up his bow and aimed an arrow at something in the area just off to my left. I clenched my fist, frustrated I couldn't see what had their attention.

My body jerked the second he released the arrow. The natives cheered, and they all walked out of sight.

"What are you doing?" Ryder said, his eyebrows pinched together as he grabbed my arm roughly. "Stay back."

"Sorry," I said, bowing my head as I rubbed my elbow.

He shook his head and glanced at the others. His shoulders sank as his cheeks turned ruby red. "I just don't want anything to happen to you, OK?"

"Sure," I said wiggling my arm until he let go. I walked back and stood in my spot, refusing to look at Shawn even though I could feel his eyes on me.

"They shot a wolf," Ryder announced. "They're dragging it behind them."

Everyone stared at Ryder waiting for more information. His head moved slowly from left to right, and then it stayed in place.

"Holy shit," Ryder said, standing as still as a statue. "They're leaving." He laughed, but his body didn't move. "They're really fucking leaving!"

He slapped his palm against his thigh and punched at the air. I wanted to smile at his enthusiastic celebration, but I couldn't.

The thought of the natives turning around and coming back for us felt far too possible. Not to mention having seen them so close to the house there was no way I'd ever feel safe at this location.

I watched the others with their big smiles and soft laughs. Charlie bounced up and down as she pumped her fist into the air almost completely silently. Logan smacked Eli on the back. They were celebrating as if we'd accomplished something major, but what had really happened was we'd gotten lucky. Very lucky.

After the brief celebration, they quickly settled. Over the next few hours we'd taken turns watching out of the window anticipating their return, but they hadn't come back.

Every time I looked out the window, all I could do was stare at the blood-streaked snow where they had dragged the dead wolf. I could still picture the arrow sticking out of the side of its neck.

They'd taken our wolf. It was probably the same one that had visited us. The one we were trying to catch.

I wondered if they were enjoying our dinner. Maybe I wouldn't have even liked wolf meat anyway.

That night I'd woke abruptly. My eyes popped wide open, and it took me a few seconds to realize where I was.

I couldn't remember exactly, but I think I'd been dreaming about the natives coming back. I sat up and looked around the room. Everyone was still asleep, all of them except for Ryder who was sitting in a chair near the window resting his face against the window frame.

"You OK?" he asked softly.

I nodded and walked over to him. It was unlikely that I would be able to fall back to sleep with my heart still pounding. "Just a bad dream, I guess."

"Do you have a lot of those?"

"No, not really. I don't really even remember it, but I can't shake the feeling. Anyway, I don't really want to talk about it," I said flashing him a small smile.

He smiled back. "We don't have to talk about it. We all have bad dreams and considering everything, I'm not sure it would even help to talk about them."

"Have you gotten any sleep yet?"

Ryder nodded. "A little. I don't need much. Never have."

I laughed. "Everyone needs sleep."

"Of course, I just don't need much."

We stared out the window in silence. I could hear Logan's heavy breathing behind me. It was just short of being a full-blown snore.

"When do you think we should leave?" I asked.

"In the morning... if we can," Ryder said looking over at Shawn. "We'll probably have to go slow, but I think we should move as soon as we possibly can."

"Which way did they go... the natives?"

Ryder looked off to the right. "East. But I'm not sure that matters."

I pressed my lips together. They could have turned south the second they were out of view. There was no way of knowing.

"How many natives are out there do you think?" I asked.

"In that group?"

I shook my head. "In all."

Ryder shrugged. "I don't think I could even guess."

"More or less than The Evolved?"

"I really can't say."

"But if you had to."

Ryder grinned. "Who's going to make me?"

"Me," I said, cocking my head to the side.

He laughed. "OK, OK, well, if you were holding me at gunpoint, I'd, and this is a complete guess, say there were more natives."

"Interesting."

"What? Are you going to organize them and take out The Evolved?" Ryder said raising an eyebrow.

I shrugged one shoulder. "Maybe. But then I'd be worried about the renegades."

He laughed and even though I hadn't felt like laughing, I couldn't help but smile back. Ryder's smile was contagious.

It surprised me how comfortable I felt with Ryder. There was just something about him that made me feel like I'd known him all my life.

"Hey," Ryder said taking my hand in his. He stood up and looked into my eyes. "I want to apologize for my behavior earlier. That was totally not cool. I panicked. I just worried that something might—"

"It's fine," I said feeling heat fill my cheeks.

"It's most definitely not fine. The thought of something happening to you just overwhelmed me. I wanted to get you away from the window, it was all I could think about." He shook his head and looked away for a second. "I'm not trying to make excuses, it was wrong, and I'm sorry."

I chewed my lip. "Really, it's fine. No harm done. I know you were just doing what you thought was best. No hard feelings, I promise."

"Well, I still feel like an ass. Everyone was staring at me. God only knows what they were thinking," Ryder said looking down into the empty space between us.

"They won't even remember in the morning," I said with a smile.

I suddenly became very aware of how close we were to one another. Charlie's words floated around in my head as I stared into his eyes.

The room was mostly dark except for the dim light across the room from the crackling fireplace. He took a small step forward, our bodies only inches apart.

"I know I haven't really known you long, but from the moment I saw you," he paused, "you've infiltrated my every thought."

All the moisture left my mouth. It felt like my lips were glued together. Even if I wanted to say something I wouldn't have been able to.

His lips curled slightly at the ends as he moved closer. My breath felt stuck in my throat, and my heart started to pound, hard pats against my chest.

I couldn't breathe.

I couldn't think.

"Hey," Eli said, looking at us from across the room.

I jumped back at least a foot. My hand pressed hard against my chest to hold my heart in place.

"Sorry, I can take over now," Eli said walking closer. He was eying us both suspiciously.

How long had he been watching?

What had he heard?

Had he noticed I was a complete idiot? Ryder smiled and patted Eli on the back as he stepped up to the window.

"Anything going on?" Eli asked.

"Nothing out there," Ryder said, glancing at me.

"Go on, get some rest," Eli said gesturing towards the floor with his chin. "Looks like morning isn't too far off."

I finally was able to swallow. My body started to

function normally again, although it felt as though electricity was running through my veins.

Ryder laid down in Eli's spot and watched me as I walked back to where I had been sleeping next to Shawn. His smile was gone, but we stared at each other for a moment in the darkness.

He blinked several times and then closed his eyes. There was no doubt in my mind that Ryder was tired, but even though I hated to admit it to myself, I wished Eli wouldn't have interrupted.

My heart and emotions were all over the place, but I'd be lying if I said I wasn't feeling something for him too. Whatever Ryder felt when we'd first met, whatever that feeling was… well, I had felt it too.

And now, maybe I'd never know. Maybe the moment was lost forever.

16

It had been two days since we'd left the brick house behind. The path had been clear as far as we could see. Not a single track of any kind in the snow, not even animals.

Shawn was healing rather quickly. The wound on his wrist still needed to be bandaged, but the cut near his eye was significantly improved. He still needed to hold his bad arm tight to his chest.

Everyone was mostly in good spirits. We had refilled our water bottles before we'd left the house and had enough food to last for days. It wasn't like we were able to have extravagant feasts, but we were fed.

We hadn't traveled far over the last couple days, but we'd been making progress. Everyone was still tired since we hadn't been getting nearly enough rest. Sleeping at night wasn't easy.

When I'd left my home, I don't think I had realized

what I was in for. Maybe if I had been traveling alone, I would have made it further, but if I was being honest with myself, I felt safer having the others with me. Although, every time I had that thought, I could hear my dad's words repeating in the back of my head.

The weather hadn't improved. It was still just as cold as it was the day I'd set out from my home. Walking through the wet, heavy snow was hard on our tired legs, but we kept going, and surprisingly with very few complaints.

We'd only been walking for a few hours when clouds filled the sky, blocking out the somewhat warming sun. The temperature felt as though it had dropped at least ten degrees, if not more, in a matter of minutes. All we could do was keep moving. The faster we moved the warmer we'd be.

"I hope we can find another house soon," Charlie said crossing her arms, rubbing her hands up and down to warm herself.

"That would be nice," Ryder said, his head moving side to side as he looked out at our surroundings. "But it's not something we can count on."

Just looking around the area, I could see how empty our world was. There wasn't anything around except for a few trees in front of us. Two of them bent to the side, leaning as if they'd been broken, and another had been uprooted and was lying flat on the ground.

There weren't any buildings in any direction for as far as the eye could see. It was just us. Alone.

"I wonder if it'll ever warm up," I said instantly wishing I could take the words back. It wasn't as though I'd wanted to scare anyone with the dreary possibility that we had nothing to look forward to. They didn't need to worry that we'd be stuck in the cold world forever. That was my worry, and I shouldn't have burdened the others with it.

"I think it will. It was warm before, and it'll be warm again. I don't think it can stay like this forever," Ryder said locking his eyes with mine. After a moment, he smiled, and when I didn't smile back, I was pretty sure he could instantly tell how worried I truly was.

I swallowed down my fears. They were mine, and I needed to keep it that way.

"You're probably right," I said shaking my head as if trying to disperse all the worries out of it. "I'm just tired. I mean, I know we all are, but I haven't slept very good the last few nights, if at all."

Ryder walked next to me and leaned in close. "More dreams?"

"Not that I can remember," I said keeping my gaze forward. Thoughts of what it had felt like the last time I'd been close to Ryder filled my mind.

As we drew closer to the area with the trees, I noticed black ovals that were scattered across the branches. At first I wasn't exactly sure what I was looking at. I'd thought they were nests stuck to the trees, but after about ten steps I could see they weren't nests. They were birds. Big, black, scary birds.

"You guys see those things?" I asked gesturing towards the birds. There was no way they couldn't have noticed them.

"Yeah, they're just birds," Charlie said with a shrug.

"You've seen them before?" I asked.

Ryder nodded slowly as he stared at them. "Only flying by overhead. Never perched on a branch like this, and never this many together."

Shawn stared at them, and his pace slowed. He grabbed my arm to stop me.

"Have you ever seen any?" I asked looking into his wide eyes.

"Yeah, I've seen them before," he said rubbing his hands together. His fingers were dark red from the cold. "We should try to go around."

Ryder turned to look at him. I watched as he studied Shawn's face.

"You know something about them?" Ryder asked. "Something you're not telling us?"

Shawn opened his mouth but quickly closed it when the largest bird released a loud caw and started wildly flapping its wings. All the birds perched on the trees cranked their necks to the side at nearly the same time as if they were looking at us.

"It doesn't look like there is going to be time to go around them. They already know we're here," Ryder said, his lips pressed tightly together as his eyes darted around.

"What should we do?" I asked.

Eli stepped in front of us and cocked his head to the side. "They look angry."

"Or maybe hungry," Charlie said gripping her club tighter.

"We're all hungry," Logan said stepping closer to Charlie.

There were about ten birds on the trees. They were different from any other bird I'd ever seen, although I hadn't seen many. These birds were bigger, and their feathers were blacker than the night sky. Even at our distance, I could see their sharp, hooked beaks.

They didn't look friendly. In fact, it appeared as though they hated us even though we'd done nothing.

The biggest bird flapped its wings and rose up into the sky. It circled above the other birds.

After a minute, the big bird released an ear-piercing caw that ripped through the air, and stabbed at my ears. I covered my ears the second the other birds echoed its call.

They all started flapping their wings, circling around the trees in one big group.

"I have a bad feeling about this," Eli said as we took several steps to the side, shifting our route away from the trees. If it was their territory, we didn't want it to look as though we were threatening it.

It didn't seem like it would matter. They were already pissed off.

The birds moved towards us cawing loudly as they

zipped through the air. Before we knew it, they were over our heads, circling above us.

"Shit," Ryder mumbled.

No matter where we walked, they stayed above us, going around and around. I kept my head forward, but my eyes were on them. Maybe it was crazy, but I was afraid that if I made direct eye contact with one of them, it would set them off.

"What are they doing?" Charlie said quietly.

"I don't know, but I don't like it," Ryder said lightly tugging on my jacket sleeve. "Let's just keep moving away."

He quickened the pace, and everyone moved their feet faster to keep up. The birds stayed directly over-head, our speed didn't matter. Fast or slow, whatever it was, they apparently were going to stay above us.

My heart was pounding so hard, and I think it increased a beat every time the birds completed a full circle. I could swear the largest bird directed its beady gaze at me even though I pretended not to notice.

"Maybe we should run," Shawn said shaking his head. "This is bad."

"What is it you aren't telling us," Ryder said increasing our speed once again.

"I wasn't sure at first, but these aren't your ordinary birds," Shawn said looking up at the sky. The big, black bird seemed to look right at him as it let out a squawk. It was like the bird was threatening him, warning him that if he didn't keep his mouth shut something bad would happen. But surely that was just my imagination.

"What are they then?" Logan asked.

Shawn looked as though he didn't want to say anything. I wasn't sure if it was because he was afraid of what we'd think of him, or if he was afraid the birds would overhear him.

We'd probably walked at least a quarter of a mile with them directly above us. They'd caw while they circled, keeping their dark little eyes on us.

This wasn't about invading their space anymore. We weren't even close to their territory. This was about something else.

"Ugh! Go away!" I said, trying not to look at the birds. I still didn't want to make eye contact.

"They aren't doing anything to us. Maybe eventually they'll just give up and leave us alone," Ryder said, glancing at Shawn. Shawn looked right back at him, his eyes wide.

Ryder was right about the fact that they weren't doing anything to us. It was just frightening and freaky to have them flying over us... watching us. As long as they didn't do anything, maybe it didn't matter?

"Maybe they are escorting us?" Charlie said, her voice wavering.

"Can they hear us?" I whispered to Shawn. He looked at me, and at first I thought he was going to think I was crazy, but then he shrugged.

"They've been modified. I don't really know much about them," Shawn whispered back.

The large bird's head twisted and looked right at Shawn. It squawked loudly and swooped down toward Shawn's head.

Charlie screamed and the big bird zipped back up into the sky with the rest of the birds.

"Jesus Christ!" Logan said.

"What the hell was that about?" Charlie screeched.

My pulse quickened. I didn't know what we could do.

"I really don't like birds," Charlie said, and several of the birds squawked. It was almost as if they were laughing.

The second they stopped making noise, a second bird swooped down toward Eli. I ducked down and covered my head.

"Give me your club," Ryder said stretching his hand out toward Charlie. "And get down."

After the third one swooped down through the middle of our group, Shawn put his good arm over my head protectively.

Ryder lifted the club. "If there's anything I need to know, Shawn, now is the time."

Shawn shook his head. "I'm sorry. I wish I knew more."

"All right then. Protect yourselves," he said holding the bat just above his shoulder. He was ready to swing at the next one that swooped.

Eli and Logan held out their small blades, but I could see the fear in their eyes. They didn't think the blades would be good enough, and quite frankly, neither did I.

One of the birds screeched loudly, and I shivered. My blood felt ice cold as it pumped quickly through my body.

I looked up and saw the black wings spread out widely a few feet away. The bird was coming right for me.

17

I heard a mushy thud, instantly followed by the sound of something crunching when the club made contact with one of the birds. There were droplets of blood on the sleeve of my jacket and on the snow around me.

"Oh, God!" I said feeling a tightening in my stomach. I swallowed hard, hoping nothing was attempting to come up.

Charlie screamed. "Get it off me! Get it off me!"

I turned to the side just as the big bird perched on her back pecked at her shoulder.

"Owww!" she cried out.

I looked up at Ryder who was already swinging at another that was heading right for her. Shawn jumped up and grabbed the bird with his bare hands. He held it awkwardly because of the sling, but still managed to twist its neck sharply to the side.

Shawn grabbed the back of Charlie's jacket and yanked her closer. He put his arm over both Charlie and I as best as he could. He rounded his back as if he was our shelter.

"Ugh," Shawn grunted. I could tell by the jerking motion of his body, he'd been pecked just like Charlie had been. "Fuck, that hurts!"

"Tell me about it," Charlie said, a tear rolled down her cheek and fell into the snow.

I couldn't see what was happening, but I heard several thuds and a painful squawk. Seconds later, there was a small chorus of caws that sounded like they were getting quieter and quieter.

My eyes slowly shifted upward, and I saw the black birds flapping their wings hard up in the sky. They were leaving.

I moved out of Shawn's protective cover and stood up. We were surrounded by the carnage of the attack. There were six bird carcasses lying in the blood sprinkled snow.

I looked at Ryder, who was still breathing heavily. There were red spots sprinkled on his face and arms.

"Are you hurt?" I asked. Ryder shook his head.

I looked at Logan who was in the middle of pulling his blade out of one of the dead birds. Both he and Eli looked like they managed to avoid injury.

"They got Charlie just once and Shawn too," I said looking at the hole in the back of Charlie's jacket.

"Twice," Shawn said pressing his hand against the

bicep on his arm that was still healing from his last injury. He opened his fingers and looked at the blood covering the center of his palm. "Any more band-aids in that handy little kit of yours?"

I nodded and unzipped my backpack. If I kept having to use my first aid kit as frequently as I had been, it wasn't going to last long.

"Bandage them up quickly," Ryder said. He was trying to look in every direction at once to make sure the birds hadn't changed their minds about leaving.

Eli stood next to me and held out his hand. I gave him one of the larger bandages, and he started helping Charlie wiggle her arm out of her jacket so he could patch up her back.

Shawn's eyes were on me as I unzipped his jacket. "Maybe you should save those. The bleeding will stop."

I looked up at him and swallowed hard. Those eyes. Those damn eyes.

"Do you even have blood left to lose?" I asked, my voice soft.

"Hurry," Ryder said.

My fingers trembled as I carefully pulled down Shawn's jacket. The wound on his bicep was a small hole with blood slowly leaking out of it.

I pressed the bandage down, feeling his warm breath against the side of my neck. My eyes shifted upward and locked with his. We were so close, and both quite aware of that fact.

"Where's the other one?" I said feeling breathless.

"My back," he said leaning closer for a second before turning around and lifting his jacket and shirt.

He hadn't lifted it high enough, but the blood dripping down his side helped me find the wound. It looked a bit worse than the one on his arm, but it didn't look serious.

"How does it look, doc?" he said over his shoulder.

"I think you'll pull through." The memory of when we'd found him lying in the snow only days ago slammed into my mind. "This is nothing compared to what you've already been through."

I pulled down his shirt and jacket. The others were standing there watching us, waiting for us to finish so we could leave the bird graveyard behind. I put away the first aid kit and zipped up my backpack.

"Ready," I said.

"About time," Charlie said, her bloodied club back in her hand.

I rolled my eyes at her the second she turned around to follow Ryder. Shawn chuckled.

He leaned closer. "She really doesn't like you."

"Shh!" I said, flashing him a big smile. He couldn't have been more right, but I didn't want to deal with a big confrontation if she or the others overheard his comment.

As we walked, Ryder's speed seemed to increase. The others kept up with him, but I stayed back with Shawn.

It seemed as though Ryder had forgotten that Shawn was still healing. Or maybe he didn't care.

Every so often he'd look over his shoulder, probably to make sure we were still with them. He didn't wait for us to catch up, he kept going.

"Bet he's trying to find a shelter before night," Shawn said.

"Probably." I looked out around us, but it was just as barren as ever. "So… about those birds?"

Shawn rubbed his bicep and sighed. "Like I said before, I don't know much about them." He looked into my eyes without blinking. "If I knew anything I'd tell you."

"You said they were modified?"

"Yeah."

"In what way?"

He shook his head. "I don't know exactly. It was some kind of science experiment, at least that's what I'd heard. Something that they'd done before I was born."

"I see." My parents had mentioned dogs that could spread diseases, but I thought they were just stories to keep me inside.

Maybe they weren't just stories. I looked at Shawn, and chewed my lip.

"What's wrong?" he asked, matching my expression.

"Are you feeling OK?"

"Yeah, why wouldn't I be?"

I adjusted my backpack which suddenly felt too

heavy. We were walking way too fast, even for me.

"Want me to carry that for a while?"

I shook my head.

Shawn seemed fine. It didn't seem like he was getting sick or anything like that, but maybe the disease my parents told me about didn't happen that quickly. Dammit! Why hadn't I paid more attention to those stories?

"Do you feel normal?" I asked looking him up and down.

"Yeeeeessss?" He narrowed his eyes at me. "What's going on, Emery?"

"Nothing."

"You're lying."

I let out a long sigh and blinked slowly. "It's nothing, really, I don't want to freak you out."

"I can handle it. Just tell me what's on your mind."

"Ugh, fine." I brushed my hands together as if I was dusting them off. "When I was younger, my parents used to tell me stories about diseased dogs. They called them dog-beasts. I don't remember much about the stories other than the dogs were dangerous. If you were bitten, you'd die."

Shawn nodded. "I know of the dogs. Never seen one though. What does this have to do with anything?"

"Probably nothing. I was just worried about what these modified birds did to you and Charlie. Hoping it's not something like the weird dogs."

"Hmm," Shawn said looking forward. He shrugged.

"I feel fine, but if anything changes, you'll be the first to know."

I pressed my lips together and nodded. Unfortunately, that hadn't made me feel any better. I was still worried.

"I think they had trouble with the birds. I'd heard they'd killed a bunch of them, but clearly, they are still out here surviving in this shit."

"Who killed them?" I asked already guessing at the answer.

"The Evolved. I think before they were even called that."

My head bobbed slowly. I already had figured it had been The Evolved. A failed experiment.

"The ones out here are probably breeding. Not much can be done about that," Shawn said looking up at the sky. "Can you imagine if you were out here alone and you didn't have a club like Charlie's? Those things could easily take a person out."

I swallowed hard. If I had kept on going alone, maybe back where the birds had attacked us, would have been where my dead body would have been lying.

"Let's just hope we don't run into them again," Shawn said as he placed his hand on my shoulder.

I didn't look at him even though I knew he was looking at me. Those eyes. I just couldn't.

"Even though I wish I could have done more to help the others, I'm glad I got out of there when I did," Shawn said. I could hear the sadness in the voice as if he were somehow blaming the bird attack partially on himself.

"Do you think they're still looking for you?" I asked.

He shook his head. "No, not really. But if we run into a base or others, they'll kill me. I'm sure of that."

"Well, won't they kill us too?"

"Maybe. Probably not. At least not at first. They'll take you and see if they can use you in some way, convert you." He leaned closer. "Especially you because of your lack of marks. But me," he pointed to the marks on his neck, "they'll consider me a traitor."

Ryder and the others were marked too but they weren't marked in the same way Shawn was. There markings were a bit more discreet, whereas Shawn's were bold and hard to miss.

"What about them?" I gestured forward with my chin.

He blew out a puff of air. "It could go either way. Depends on how much of a fight they put up."

They'd put up a fight. No question about it.

"Wooo hooo!" Ryder shouted from farther ahead than the last time I looked. He was pumping his fists into the air while the others hopped around.

"What's going on?" Shawn asked.

"No idea," I said looking around. I had been spending most of my time staring at my feet, or up at the sky for birds to notice what they'd seen. But after I blinked a few times, I smiled when I noticed. I grabbed Shawn's hand. "Let's go!"

Even though everyone was tired, we all ran towards the two-story brick house. It would be night soon, so the temperature was dropping rapidly.

It was hard to be sure, but the house looked as though it was in solid condition. All four walls were there, and the roof was still on top, we couldn't have asked for anything better. It was nothing short of a miracle.

Ryder ran up the steps to the porch and peered in the window. He waved at us before disappearing inside. Eli and Logan followed close behind.

Charlie wasn't far behind, but she was dragging her feet a bit more. I could tell she was worn out, and I imagined her wound probably wasn't helping matters.

By the time Shawn and I got inside, the others had already looked through the house. Ryder gave the all clear that no one was inside.

It was significantly darker inside than it had been outside. Any light that had been peeking through the clouds was fading away quickly.

Logan moved his hand around inside the fireplace and cursed as he punched the air. He didn't even need to say anything, it was obvious there was no wood for a fire.

In fact, the last time we'd even seen any wood had been back where the birds had attacked us. Maybe there would be something in the house we'd be able to burn.

"I have a blanket," I said, as if that somehow helped.

The others started looking around the house, but the doors, cabinets, and anything that had been made of wood had been stripped out. By the looks of it, it had happened a long time ago too.

It was going to get awfully cold in the house without a fire. In fact, it would probably be too cold. Even when we had to be outside, we'd have a fire. We needed something more than a couple blankets to keep us warm during the night.

"Can we stay?" I asked.

Ryder shook his head. "Who knows if we'd find anything out there either."

"I'll go check around," Logan said and left the house.

Ryder glanced at Eli. Eli nodded before he went after Logan.

"Look around to see if there's anything we can

burn," Ryder said, but he was already shaking his head. "Dammit! There has to be something."

Unlike the last house we'd stayed at, this one was completely empty. No debris. No junk. No trash. Nothing. Just four walls and the plastered ceiling.

"What about the floorboards?" I asked.

"I'm not sure," Ryder said.

Charlie came down the stairs carrying two small blankets. "These should help a little."

"I'm surprised you found anything," I said, taking my blanket out from my backpack.

"Me too," she said. "They were shoved at the back of a linen closet. They kind of stink."

Shawn spun around in a slow circle. "I've never seen anything like this. I can't believe they took everything."

The doors had been ripped off their hinges. Shelving and cabinets ripped off the walls. Everything that had been inside was gone.

"Maybe whoever was here needed to burn it," Ryder said.

"They should have torn up the floors," Shawn said with a small shrug.

Ryder cocked his head to the side. "Maybe they'd left."

"Or maybe someone came here and collected the wood... brought it somewhere else to build something entirely new," Charlie said tapping her finger against her lip.

"It's not really a mystery we need to solve. It's gone," I said, and Charlie sneered at me.

Ryder looked at the stairs. "I guess we could start with the stairs, or maybe the upstairs floorboards."

"How are you going to get it out? With your bare hands?" I asked.

Ryder shrugged. "I don't know it was your idea!"

The front door opened and everyone turned, looking hopefully at Logan and Eli. It was obvious from their somber expressions that they hadn't found anything.

Ryder, Logan, and Eli talked about the stairs and floorboards while Charlie and I arranged the sleeping area. We'd lay side by side like sardines, which would hopefully help keep us warm.

"We'll be OK," Ryder said sitting down in the middle of the blankets. "Let's eat something and rest. I'm too tired to think straight. We'll figure something out."

We sat down in a row and ate a small ration. There was still food left, we would be OK for a while, but it wasn't going to last forever. We were going to need to find a food source sooner or later, but now probably wasn't the best time to bring it up.

"Maybe we should have kept some of those birds," I said swallowing down a small drink.

"I doubt you'd want to eat those things," Shawn mumbled.

He had a point.

After everyone was done eating, Ryder announced that we'd all take turns keeping watch. Eli volunteered to go first. Ryder wanted him to alternate between the front window and the back window, trying to keep an eye in all directions.

As long as there was some moonlight, we'd be able to see something coming. But, there probably wasn't anyone that would be out traveling at night in the cold unless they absolutely had to. Even the natives with their animal furs on their back wouldn't be out traveling in the frigid conditions.

We hadn't seen anyone around since we'd seen the natives. They were probably somewhere warm, feasting on wolf meat.

Eli sat at the window while the rest of us laid down close together. The blankets were perfectly spread out so that everyone was covered.

"It's not so bad," Charlie said. She was to my left between Ryder and Logan.

It wasn't bad at least for me, Ryder and Charlie. Eli at the window and those on the ends might disagree.

I was tucked snuggly between Ryder and Shawn. My face was cold, but my body was warm.

"Who needs a fire?" Ryder joked smiling in the darkness.

"I'd be happy with a fire, and even a couple more blankets," I said smiling back.

It didn't take long, once we all settled down, for everyone to fall asleep. Everyone but me.

I tossed and turned for what felt like hours. Every time I tried to close my eyes, they'd pop open seconds later.

I was still awake when Logan took over on watch. Logan grimaced as he walked by noticing me watching him move about.

"Go to sleep," he whispered.

I frowned at him. "I wish I could!"

I felt tired. My body was exhausted, but I couldn't fall asleep. At least I wasn't keeping the others awake with my constant moving around.

Ryder turned on his side and looked at me. "He's right. You need to sleep. Just close your eyes and try to relax."

"Obviously, that's what I've been trying to do."

Ryder took my hand in his and softly stroked the back of it with his thumb. I closed my eyes, but a few minutes later, they popped back open.

When I closed my eyes, I'd see the birds circling overhead, or I'd imagine the natives walking up to the house pounding on the doors and windows until they broke. I couldn't relax. It just wasn't an option.

"Your heart's beating so fast," Ryder said. "What are you thinking about?"

"All the things that could go wrong," I replied.

Ryder moved a bit closer. "You can't let yourself think about that stuff. It'll eat away at you until it paralyzes you with fear. What happened to that tough girl that rescued me? The girl that was going to go south all by herself?"

He smiled at me, but it quickly faded when he realized I wasn't going to smile back. Ryder was right though, that girl wasn't here anymore.

Somehow, I'd changed. Maybe it was because I'd lost hope. I'd seen the world for what it really was. A giant, white, ice cold graveyard.

I wasn't safe anymore. I wasn't warm and cozy with my family. Out here, I was alone, and seemingly in constant danger. The outside world had changed from what my parents had described. If only they would have known, they would have given me different advice.

"Please, try not to worry," Ryder said looking into my eyes. "I'll keep you safe. We'll all look out for each other. It's going to be OK. We'll get through this."

I stared into his eyes. It felt nice to hear the words, but I wanted to be able to take care of myself. I didn't want to have to rely on others because that didn't last forever. One day those you loved and cared about were just... gone.

Maybe it was weird, but my dad had trained me for this life. I could take care of myself, at least I thought I had been able to, but now that I was being tested, it was almost as if I was too afraid to do it.

I wouldn't be able to battle the natives on my own. I wouldn't have even survived the bird attack. My dad hadn't warned me about those things. I could use the gun, and I was a good shot. I knew how to find food and water, but I didn't know the first thing about taking out a group of killer birds.

If I had listened to his advice, I wouldn't be with Ryder, Shawn, or the others. I wished I could tell him he'd been wrong. That there were still good, caring people out there.

"Yeah. We'll take care of each other," I whispered, and Ryder smiled. I wanted the words to be true.

"Sounds perfect."

He inched his lips closer and closer. It felt as though my heart had stopped. Before I knew it, my eyes were closed, and his lips were pressed against mine.

My body relaxed as our lips moved together. His mouth was warm and his lips soft. It was like a dream.

I pressed my hand against his chest, and he eased back. He looked down at my lips, need filled his eyes. I knew why he'd stopped.

Neither of us wanted it to end, but it had too. We weren't alone. Anyone could wake up at any moment. He had to stop while he could still control himself.

My thoughts went to Shawn. What would he have thought if he would have seen us? Why would it have mattered?

Shawn was my friend.

My friend with the hypnotizing eyes. That's all he was. A friend. A good friend. I barely knew him. Was he even a friend? I didn't know what he was, or why I was even thinking about him.

Ryder didn't let go of my hand. He sucked in a deep breath and released air slowly between his slightly parted lips. I watched his chest rise and fall over and over again until my eyes closed.

My breathing mirrored Ryder's, and it didn't take long before I was asleep. When my eyes opened again, Ryder was standing at the window releasing a stream of curses.

Logan was pacing, running his hands through his hair. Shawn was sitting up watching them with wide eyes as he massaged his bicep just below where the bird had pecked him.

"What's going on?" I whispered.

Shawn turned to me and swallowed hard. "It's snowing."

19

Snowing? The way they were all staring out the window made me really worried. It must have been bad.

I held my breath as I got up and exhaled slowly as I walked over to the window. With each step, it felt like pins and needles poked into my feet. I reached up and pulled back the curtain. Everything outside the window was white as if someone was holding a piece of paper up against the glass. Thick, white flakes fell from the sky and covered the ground like a fluffy, freezing cold blanket. Visibility was low. I couldn't see much beyond the front porch.

"We need to figure out how to get something going in this fireplace," Ryder said looking around. Hopefully, they'd be able to find some wood now that it was lighter out than when we'd first arrived.

Ryder elbowed Logan, and they started wandering

around the house. It wasn't long before I heard pounding in one of the other rooms.

Charlie was sitting on the floor hugging her knees. Her lips were deep shade of dark purple, and she was shivering. The cocky attitude she once had, was completely gone. I wished she would have stayed back with Jacob. I wished they all would have.

Ryder and Logan came back into the room with two long wooden boards. Logan set Charlie's club against the wall. A few of the nails were bent. They must have bashed something until they were able to get the wood free.

"What did you do?" Eli asked, as Logan cracked the boards over his knee and tossed the wood into the fireplace.

"Broke through the wall," Logan said shaking his head. "It's colder in there. I'm not sure that was a smart move considering the lack of a door, not to mention the fact that we can't burn the house down around us."

Once the fire was going, the room warmed rather quickly. No one really talked. Everyone had their mind on what was happening outside.

The weather wasn't improving and maybe it never would. In fact, it was getting worse.

Each time it snowed it got harder and harder to survive. The trees and plants didn't grow back. Animals and people died out. Eventually, there wouldn't be anything left. Maybe this was it for us.

Maybe it was our last snow storm and that thought was probably weighing heavily on everyone's mind.

Ryder stared out the window, but I knew he couldn't see anything but a sheet of snow. No doubt he was lost in his thoughts just like the others were.

I stepped up next to him. He hadn't seemed to notice I was there until I lightly touched his arm.

Ryder swallowed and wrapped his arm around my waist. He took a deep breath and leaned his head against my arm. He didn't say anything, but I could tell he was terrified of what the snow falling meant for our future.

I was sure the others had their eyes on us, but I didn't care. I combed my fingers through his hair. After a moment he sniffed hard and straightened his spine. His eyes focusing on the snow outside, acting as if nothing had happened.

"You OK?" I said in a quiet voice.

He nodded. "We'll be fine. It's going to be fine."

It didn't seem as if he believed his own words. He was saying them for my benefit... hoping that I'd believe them, but of course, I didn't.

"Look over there!" I said pointing through the falling snow. I saw something moving. It was close enough that I could see the gray tones standing out against all the falling snow. "And there!"

"Wolves!" Ryder said turning around toward the others. They didn't move. His eyes met mine. "We have to figure out a way."

I nodded. "Charlie's club. They won't see us coming."

Ryder stood up, taking big steps across the room. He picked up Charlie's club with a big grin on his face. The others finally shifted their eyes upward and took notice.

"What's going on?" Logan asked as he pulled back his shoulders.

"Wolves. And I'm going to catch us one for dinner," Ryder said as he quietly opened the door and stepped outside.

He left the door open a crack, probably because he didn't want to make any noise that might scare the wolves away. The snow on the concrete porch crunched under his boots as he took carefully calculated steps.

The nearest wolf stopped digging its snout in the snow and looked up. Ryder held absolutely still. The wolf looked around and then took three steps before digging into the snow again.

Ryder started moving again. He crept closer and closer. Every time the wolf paused, Ryder froze. It was like they were playing a game, and Ryder was more than determined to win.

He slowly raised up the club and took three quick steps forward, putting all his weight behind his swing. The wolf whimpered and fell to the ground. It whined, and Ryder lifted the club again. I stepped away from the door and sat near the fire.

I didn't need to see.

He'd killed it.

There was a loud howl, followed by Ryder shouting something. Logan went flying out of the door.

"What happened?" I asked knowing full well the others sitting with me had no idea.

I bolted to the door, placing my hands on either side of the door frame as I peered out into the snow. White. Everything was white. I couldn't see anything, except the falling snow.

"Ryder!" I shouted.

My eyes darted around trying to find movement. Something. Had that been something to my right?

I peered into the falling white fluffs as I stepped out of the house into the snowstorm without my jacket. "Ryder!"

My heart was racing. Where was he? Why wasn't he answering?

I kept walking forward until something grabbed my arm and pulled me back. A hand clamped down over my mouth before I was able to scream.

"It's just me," Shawn said slowly pulling his hand away. "What are you doing?"

"I'm looking for…."

Seconds later, Ryder and Logan stepped out of the whiteness dragging a wolf behind them. Ryder glared at Shawn.

"What is she doing out here?" Ryder asked as if he thought Shawn had been to blame.

"I don't know. She went after you I guess," Shawn said.

"I'm right here," I said between my teeth. My eyes locked with Ryder's. "I heard you shouting. I was worried."

"The second one tried to attack him when he killed the first," Logan said.

I swallowed hard. "Oh, I... are you OK?"

"I'm fine," Ryder said. "Unfortunately, the other one got away."

"This will be enough," Logan said, as he and Ryder pulled the dead wolf through the snow toward the house.

I shivered, and Shawn put his arm around me. "Let's go inside," he said, rubbing my arm vigorously with his hand. "It's freezing out here."

I nodded as he led me inside. My body felt stiff. I wasn't sure if it was because of the cold or if it had been due to the fear that something had happened to Ryder.

Maybe it had been both.

The second we were in the house I stepped away from Shawn. I could feel his eyes on me as I walked over to the fire.

What was wrong with me?

I had set out determined to do this on my own, but after everything, I wasn't even sure I could do this with the others by my side. If I lost them, I'd give up, and I think that thought terrified me even more.

I sat down close to the fire, but it didn't seem to be warming my body. It felt as though my bones were made of ice. I was being frozen from the inside out.

I jumped when someone touched my shoulder. Ryder was standing behind me, gesturing for me to follow. Shawn's eyes shifted up toward me, but he quickly looked away as Ryder led me out of the room.

We stood there in the freezing room they'd taken wood from staring at each other. After a second he stepped forward and pulled me into his arms.

It seemed as though he didn't know what to say and neither had it. Being in his arms instantly helped warm my bones.

"I was worried," I finally said after he held me for several minutes.

"For a second, I was too," he said with a smile.

I pulled back slightly so I could look into his eyes. "What happened?"

"The other one jumped on me. Knocked me to the ground. I swung at him but missed. He howled and ran away. Logan helped me up, and that's when I saw you were standing out there trying to catch your death."

Ryder placed his hand on the back of my neck. His head moved side to side like a pendulum.

"You shouldn't have gone out there," he said pressing his lips to my forehead.

"I thought something happened to you."

He put his thumb on my chin and raised my face, so I was forced to look into his eyes. "Even if something

163

happens to me, you have to keep going. You can't put yourself in danger for any reason. Ever. Promise?"

I nodded, but I wasn't sure his words had sunk in. Even if they had, I didn't know what I would or wouldn't do if something happened to him. How could I go on? How could any of us?

It would just be a sign of how limited our time was for all of us. First one and then the next. That's how it would be.

"Look," Ryder said, smiling, "everything is fine. I'm OK, you're OK, and now we have food."

"You shouldn't have gone out there either. I couldn't see anything. I don't even know how Logan found you." I shook my head. "He could have gotten lost. You both could have."

Ryder tightened his arms around me, but he didn't say anything. Hopefully, that was because he'd already known it hadn't been the smartest move. Or maybe it was because he would have done it again in a heartbeat.

"Are you going to be OK?"

I nodded.

"I'm going to help Logan clean the wolf. Stay inside?"

"I can help," I said. It was true. I could. I'd seen my dad skin various small animals.

He flashed me a half-smile and stepped away. "I'm sure you could, but I rather you stay inside. Warm up. OK?"

I pressed my lips together and nodded. After he'd

stepped away, my bones felt cold again. I did need to warm up, but I wasn't sure if I could do it without his arms around me.

Eli worked on collecting more wood from the ceiling while Logan and Ryder worked on the wolf. Charlie, Shawn and I sat near the fire, mostly in silence.

Even while we filled our bellies with the over-cooked wolf meat, we didn't talk much. My thoughts were on the snow falling outside. There wasn't anything I could to stop thinking about it.

If it kept falling, and it didn't warm up, this brick house was where I'd die. Or maybe we'd try to travel, in which case my grave would be out in the middle of nowhere.

Perhaps everyone was trying to come to terms with the same fate.

After we'd finished, Ryder and Logan packed the leftover meat deep in a pile of snow. There was a chance something would come along and steal it, but we didn't have a whole lot of options. Hopefully, there wouldn't be anything wandering around blindly.

That night I tossed and turned more than usual. Even when Ryder held my hand, I couldn't fall asleep. I didn't want to face the nightmares. The one I was living in was bad enough.

When the house lit up some, I knew it was morning. I could tell without getting up that the sun wasn't shining. What I didn't know was if the snow was still falling.

I got up and slowly walked to the window while the others slept. Eli was at the back window, and I could sense his eyes on me, but he didn't say anything.

I held my breath as I pulled back the curtain.

20

G od dammit.

It was still snowing. I watched as it dropped down to the ground, trying to decide if it had let up. Eli stepped up behind me, and my body jerked.

"Sorry," he whispered. He must have been trying not to wake the others.

"For startling me, or because it's still snowing?"

"Only sorry for the one that's my fault," Eli said with a grin.

I sucked in a deep breath, my shoulders sinking down as I released it. "Do you think it's less than yesterday?"

He tilted his head slightly. "Maybe? It's hard to say, but I can tell it's still just as cold."

"How do you know that?"

"I can feel it when I step into the other room. It's so

cold in there, and the more wood we pull out, the colder it's getting. If this weather doesn't change—"

"I know. It's not good," I said, my lip trembling ever so slightly. "You don't need to remind me."

Eli frowned. "Sorry." He hesitated. "For the reminder."

I pressed my hands against my face. Eli's footsteps lightly tapped against the floor as he walked to the back of the house. I reached over and grabbed my jacket to keep myself warm as I stared out the window.

My eyes shifted their focus to the front door, moving down until they settled on the doorknob. Maybe I should walk out there... just keep walking. Take matters into my own hands instead of sitting around waiting for death to find me.

"Good morning," Ryder said, placing his hands on my shoulders. My visions of walking away poofed away like someone had poked a balloon with a pin. "Damn. Still snowing, huh?"

I nodded.

Ryder crouched down next to the chair and leaned in close. "It's going to be OK. We'll figure it out. For now, we're safe in here... just think if we hadn't found this place."

"That's supposed to make me feel better?" I asked.

"I'm not sure what it was supposed to do." Ryder smiled.

I forced a smile back, but I could tell by the twitch near the corner of his eyes that he could see right through my attempt. His cold fingers slid around the side of my neck, turning me so he could look into my eyes.

"Things could be so much worse. We have food, water, and a shelter—"

"The second we can't put wood in that fireplace, we'll start dying. It might not happen quickly, but it'll happen."

"We don't know that," Ryder said, his jaw tensing. "There is still wood in this house we can use before we even have to start worrying."

I shifted my weight and stared right back. "If the snow doesn't stop—"

"It will stop."

"You don't know that."

He shook his head. "Of course I don't, but I haven't given up since the second I was born. I'm not about to give up now. I've been through far worse than this."

"I haven't." My gaze shifted away from his.

"Is that right?"

He was challenging me. I could tell by his tone. Ryder was right. I'd been through worse, and he was calling me out on it. First I'd lost my dad, and not even that long ago, my mom. Somehow, I'd survived that. Of course, he was right... but it was hard to think about it the way he did. Each snowflake that fell was a minute being shaved off my life, and there a lot of snowflakes falling.

"Want to help me prepare some breakfast?" he asked as he stood and held out his hand.

"Sure," I said slipping my hand into his.

"Let's go see if our food is still buried in the snow."

I pulled on my hat and gloves and followed Ryder out of the house. The cold air against my face felt like sharp pins pricking at my cheeks. Even with the instant chill, it felt good to be out of the house. I couldn't dwell on all the negative things I'd been focusing on because the only thing I could think about outside was how ungodly cold it was.

"Brrr!" I said, and Ryder put his arm around me. His cheeks were dark pink from the cold, but there was a sparkle in his eye. "You're crazy."

"A little," he said sliding his hand around the back of my neck. He pulled me closer and kissed me. "But only in the good way."

His lips were soft and warm. Heat surged through my veins, as the snow fell down on us. The air was bitterly cold, but I felt as though I was melting into Ryder.

He pulled back, and I couldn't help but smile at him. Ryder took my hand into his and led me to the side of the house where there was a big pile of undisturbed snow.

"Good. It's still here," he said, bending down to dig into the pile. "When I was younger, we used to have potatoes. I miss potatoes."

"My mom had a garden for a while." I could barely

remember it. It was a memory that seemed to have stayed back at the house with her.

I remembered the seeds I had with me. If we could ever find warmth, soil, and water we'd be able to have fresh fruits and vegetables. Potatoes. But I didn't mention the seeds.

"That must have been nice," Ryder said.

I nodded as he pulled out a big slab of meat and set it down in the clean white snow. He covered up what remained, packing the snow around it tightly before picking up the meat.

"What about all that? Won't it draw attention?" I asked pointing at the bloody snow with my boot.

"Maybe, but it'll be covered up in no time. I think it'll be OK," Ryder said.

A wolf let out a loud, sharp howl and we both turned sharply to the right. I didn't see anything, but it hadn't sounded as though it was too far from where we were.

"He hates me," Ryder said grabbing my hand, leading me back to the front of the house.

My eyes darted around looking for the wolf. It howled again, and I was certain it was even closer than it had been.

"Come on," Ryder said, picking up his pace just short of a run. "Probably should have taken the club."

I took off my glove and tucked it into my pocket. My hand resting on the cold metal at the back of my hip. It would be sorry if it messed with me.

———

It was around midday when Ryder pulled me into the back room where they had been pulling wood from. If anyone noticed us sneaking away, they hadn't said anything.

"What is it?" I said, not understanding the look on Ryder's face. I narrowed my eyes expecting to be hit with a brick of bad news.

"You look so worried," he said stepping closer. Heat seemed to radiate out of his eyes. "I just wanted to spend some time with you. Distract you."

Thankfully I had my jacket on, it was practically a requirement in the back room. I stuffed my hands into my pockets to keep them warm.

"What will the others think?" I said wearing a sly, little smirk.

"Who cares?" Ryder said flashing a smirk of his own right back at me.

He took another step towards me, and I took one back. The look in his eyes was burning hotter than the fire in the other room. It was a bit overwhelming.

My back bumped into the wall behind me, and a tiny gasp escaped from between my lips. The pounding in my chest was like a low, rhythmic drum beat.

Bump… bump… bump.

Ryder put his hand up against the wall on my right, and then on my left. He stared at my lips.

"What has gotten into you?" I said in an airy voice.

"I just realized something today," he said moving his lips closer to my ear.

I swallowed down the lump that had formed in the back of my throat. "What's that?"

"That I don't want to waste any time." His lips lightly brushed against the skin just below my ear. I felt his breath dance down my neck. "Do you?"

I shivered and shook my head.

It was true. I didn't want to waste time either, but that didn't ease my nerves. It wasn't as though I was about to admit it to Ryder, but I had no experience with anything like this. I didn't know how to act. Or even what I should say.

"I didn't think so," Ryder said, kissing down my neck hungrily. My entire body felt as though it was on fire. And there was one thing I knew for certain... that I didn't want him to stop.

Ryder slid his hand around the back of my neck and tilted my head upward. He kissed me hard, our mouths moving together perfectly with a need I couldn't control.

I pressed my hand against his chest as his fingertips glided down my shoulder. He stopped at the zipper on my jacket. I could feel his lips curl into a sinful smile.

I drew in a sharp breath when he pulled the zipper down and the cool air brushed against my skin His hand slid around my waist, and he pulled my body tightly to his.

I copied what he'd done and unzipped his jacket. My heart racing as I placed my palm on his solid chest.

Ryder pressed his body harder against mine, and I could feel just how badly he wanted me. He leaned into me, moving his knee between my legs as his hand slid inside my shirt.

"Mmm." My voice was soft, barely noticeable. His touch felt amazing.

Ryder gazed into my eyes, and when I smiled, he smiled back. Our hands moved everywhere at once. Exploring every inch of one another.

I didn't want the moment to ever end. It was the first time since leaving my home, I hadn't been worried about something. Being with Ryder felt so right.

His abs tightened when I slid my hand inside his shirt. My cool fingers glided over his silky-smooth skin. I loved how he felt both soft and hard at the same time.

Ryder's hand moved up my side. The second he touched my breast, I gasped.

"Ohhh," I said, biting my lip to stop any other sounds from leaking out.

Ryder smiled. His lips quickly found mine again.

The floorboards creaked behind Ryder, and my eyes popped open. It was strange how the small noise had cut through the quiet like a razor blade.

"What's wrong?" he asked looking into my eyes as I stood on my tip-toes and looked over his shoulder.

My eyes locked with Charlie's for a split-second.

Ryder turned abruptly to see what had grabbed my attention, but before he'd even been able to turn, she was running from the doorway.

"What was that about?" Ryder said, his eyes still on the space where the door would have been.

"Charlie." I paused. "I… I don't really know," I said pulling my jacket closed, suddenly realizing how cold the room was. Or because of how little privacy we really had.

Seconds later, there was a loud bang. It sounded like the front door being slammed shut.

"God dammit!" Ryder said turning to me. "You OK?"

I nodded. "Yeah, I'm fine."

He kissed my cheek. "I'll be back. Don't go outside."

Ryder ran from the room, and I followed him. Logan was standing in the doorway looking outside. I could see the snow was still falling outside, but it seemed as though it had let up.

"She ran out," Logan said glancing at Ryder. "Eli went after her. Know what that was all about?"

Ryder shook his head.

Shawn was standing near the fire looking back and forth between the front door and me. It was clear he had no idea what had just happened.

I wasn't even sure if Ryder knew exactly what had happened. But I knew. Charlie had seen us. She'd seen Ryder kissing me, and she ran away. She couldn't get away fast enough.

"They went that way," Logan pointed. Ryder nodded and stared out the door as if he could see them.

"I'll go after them," Ryder said as he pulled on his hat and gloves. "Stay here with them."

"Ryder," I said taking in a quick breath. I didn't want him to go. He'd get lost out there.

He looked at me without blinking. "I'll be back. I promise. Stay with Logan."

I shook my head and took a quick step toward him. But before I could say anything, he was gone.

21

I walked over to the window and watched Ryder running away until I couldn't see him any longer. I could feel Logan's eyes on me.

"What happened?" he asked when our eyes connected.

I didn't know what to say. I hesitated so long he looked away from me.

"She... I guess maybe she didn't like—"

"There's Ryder!" Logan said, and I saw the movement. He was carrying something... someone. Eli.

Where was Charlie?

"Help me!" Ryder shouted, and Logan ran out of the house. They noisily carried Eli into the house and laid him down on the blankets near the fire.

The second they stepped back I saw the arrow sticking out of the side of his chest. He was as white as a ghost.

"Where's Charlie?" I asked.

"Still… out… there," Eli said wincing more and more with each word.

Ryder stood up and went to the door. "Take care of him."

I wanted to run after him. Beg him to stop, but I couldn't.

Eli groaned.

Logan was kneeling next to his head looking distraught. Shawn was lightly touching Eli's jacket where the arrow had pierced through it.

"I could pull it," Shawn said looking at Logan and then at me.

I shook my head. The injury was far beyond anything I'd be able to take care of… if it was even something that could be treated at all.

"Don't pull it," Eli said between his clenched teeth. His eyes were half closed. "That'll just kill me faster."

I couldn't stop the tear that leaked out of the corner of my eye and rolled down my cheek. He knew it, just as well as I did that he wasn't going to make it.

I'd seen both my parents die, and I recognized the signs. There wasn't anything we could do to save him.

If we managed to get the arrow out, he'd bleed to death. Maybe it would be quicker, but getting the arrow out would cause him tremendous amounts of pain. It would be torture.

Eli was the one dying, he should get to choose how he wanted to leave this world. His eyes stayed closed longer and longer with each blink. He was struggling to take in each one of his breaths.

"Hey," Eli said forcing a half-smile, "it's OK.

More tears leaked out of my eyes. Logan's head was down. I knew him, and Eli had been close.

Eli's eyes were on Logan, but Logan's were focused on his knees as his shouldered bobbed up and down. It seemed to take a lot of effort, but Eli placed his hand on top of Logan's.

"This hurts like hell...," he drew in a sharp breath, "I... I can't do it. I have to go."

My hand shook as I moved it to cover my mouth. Watching someone die was something that never got easier.

"I love you, man," Logan said, and I saw Eli tap his fingers on Logan's hand three times before they stopped moving.

His whole body had stopped. He was gone.

I pulled out my knife and sawed away at the arrow. Logan reached out his hand to stop me, but Shawn pulled him back. The second Logan realized what I was doing his head dropped.

Once I had the arrow off, I covered him with one of the blankets. There wasn't anything I could say to Logan. I stood next to him and placed my hand on his shoulder for a moment before stepping away.

I sat by the window and watched for Ryder while the tears streamed down my cheeks. The snow was letting up, but still, there was no sign of Ryder or Charlie.

For all I knew, he was out there with an arrow in his chest just like the one Eli had. Only there wasn't anyone out there to carry him back.

Logan sat opposite the fire with his head down. He was like a statue. I don't think he'd moved since I'd covered Eli.

The snow had almost completely stopped, but the sun was falling down toward the horizon. If Ryder didn't make it back soon, he probably wouldn't be coming back at all.

I wanted to be angry he'd left, but he'd known Charlie all his life. He'd probably even known how she'd felt about him, even if he had ignored it. It wasn't like I'd wanted her to get hurt, and I was sure Ryder hadn't either.

"Anything?" Shawn said stepping up behind me.

I shook my head and sniffed. "Nothing."

"He'll be back," Shawn said, but he was only trying to make me feel better. "The fire's dying. Think I should try to collect some wood?"

"Hmm," I said, chewing on my fingernail. "Maybe give it a little longer."

Logan stood up and left the room. Moments later we heard the pounding.

It wasn't long before the fire was going again, and Logan slumped back down onto the floor in the same spot. Shawn paced behind me.

"What are we going to do if they don't come back," Shawn asked, stopping directly at my back where I couldn't see him.

"I don't know," I said glancing at Logan. He wasn't about to offer advice.

"Should we go out looking for them?" Shawn asked.

I shook my head. "That would just end with all of us getting lost or killed. We should wait... at least for now."

"Agreed," Shawn said, lightly placing his hand on my shoulder. "I'm sorry. I wish I knew what to say, or do for you. Both of you."

I nodded and turned away.

"Can I make you guys something to eat?" Shawn asked. Neither of us answered. I didn't think I could eat when my stomach was in knots. "I'll make something."

Through the corner of my eye, I watched him pull on his jacket. His arm had healed rather quickly. I could tell by his slow movements it wasn't back to full usage, but it was significantly better than when we'd found him.

Eli had been the one to help me patch Shawn up. And Shawn and I hadn't been able to do the same for him.

The second Shawn stepped outside, I started crying again. I tried to keep quiet since losing Eli was Logan's loss. I'd barely even known him. Logan was hurting, not that he'd ever say so. I wished I could take the pain away, but I knew that I couldn't. Nothing could.

The door burst open, and Shawn was standing there without the meat. He was breathing heavily. "They're back. They're almost back. I'm going to help. I'll be right back."

The door slammed shut, and I stood up. I walked to the door and opened it to see if I could see them. The cold air blasted me in the face so hard I had to step back. The wind was so cold it felt as though I'd been instantly frozen.

I shivered and closed the door. Before I could even grab my jacket, the door burst open again. Snow drifted in with Shawn as he stepped inside with his arm around Charlie. I sucked in the frigid air sharply when I saw Ryder on her other side.

I exhaled and took in another breath as though I was learning how to breathe for the first time. It pinched my lungs, but I breathed... and breathed.

He didn't know about Eli. Neither did Charlie.

Ryder's eyes scanned the room as if he was taking attendance. When his eyes stopped on the blanket covered body, he dropped to his knees.

22

Shawn and I moved Eli's body behind the house. We discussed it briefly, and everyone agreed it would be best to take him outside. After we covered him with snow, we waited outside for as long as we could to give Ryder, Logan, and Charlie some time alone.

When we got back inside, they were sitting in silence. It hadn't seemed as though they'd talked at all since we'd left, but then again, maybe they had just run out of things to talk about.

I sat down next to Ryder and put my arm around his waist. He rested his head against my shoulder for a second before popping it back up again.

"I should have been here," Ryder said. "Maybe I could have—"

"There wasn't anything anyone could have done," I

said, squeezing him a little tighter. "He was in a lot of pain."

Ryder sniffed hard and nodded. "I could have at least tried."

"Charlie wouldn't be back if you hadn't gone after her," I said, but it didn't seem as though my words had made him feel any better. "What happened out there anyway?"

"Natives," Ryder said, glancing at Charlie.

I looked at Charlie for maybe the first time since she'd gotten back. She was hugging herself. Her eyes were dark, and she looked different. She looked smaller and her skin pale. The spunky girl with a sharp tongue was gone.

She had been different for a while, or at least at it had seemed that way. Charlie had been getting as discouraged as the rest of us, but this was different.

"How did you get her back from them?" I asked. The room was silent except for the crackling fire.

"I cut one… knocked the other out. When I grabbed the third one's bow, he ran off," Ryder said, pausing between his words. His eyes quickly shifted towards Charlie and then back down at his hands.

"So they're still out there?"

Ryder nodded.

"Did they see which way you guys left?"

"I don't think so," Ryder said.

I glanced at Shawn, and I could tell by the look on his face that he had noticed something was odd too. It was as though there was something they weren't telling us.

Charlie was rubbing her wrists, and I could see red cuts similar to the ones Shawn had when we'd found him. "Are you sure they were natives?"

"Well, they didn't say 'hello we're natives,' but I'm pretty sure. They didn't have tattoos on their necks or faces. Why do you ask?" Ryder said meeting my eyes.

"Her wrist looks like just like Shawn's when we found him. I guess it doesn't really mean anything." I shrugged.

"She was tied," Ryder whispered, but it hadn't been quiet enough. His words had apparently aggravated Charlie.

She stood up and glared at me. "They tied me up, pulled my pants down, and did terrible things to me. I can tell you the details if you'd like. And the whole time," her hands were balled up into tight fists, "they told me how I was going back to their camp, so everyone could have a turn."

She stepped closer, showing me her blood covered wrist.

"They cut me. They hit me. All in the time I was gone. The only reason I'm alive... hell, I don't even know why I'm still alive. I wish I wasn't."

"I'm sorry." It was all I could say. I wished there had been something, but there wasn't anything I could do or say to fix what happened.

Charlie sat back down, itching her arm as if something was crawling under her skin. "They told me they're coming back for me. It was the last thing that gross one shouted before Ryder got me out of there."

"We have to get out of here," I said standing up. "Why are we even still here?"

"It's almost night," Ryder said. "There were only three of them. There are six of us."

"What if they're getting help?" I said almost shouting at him.

He swallowed hard. He was struggling with all the same things I was questioning. It wasn't like he had the answers... Ryder didn't know what to do either.

"The temperature is dropping fast. I don't think they'll be coming," he said.

"That's when they will come! When we least expect it!" I screeched.

Shawn placed his hand on my shoulder in an attempted to calm me down. I shrugged him off.

"I'm right!" I said. "We have to get her out of here!"

Logan stood up and stomped his boot loudly against the floor. My mouth snapped shut. I looked up at him, my heart pounded in my chest.

"If we go out there, we'll all end up like Eli. Is that what you want?" Logan said.

I drew in a deep breath and shook my head. My knees felt weak. I carefully lowered myself to the floor. It felt as though I just couldn't hold myself up any longer.

How would I have been able to travel in the

freezing cold in the darkness? I was completely drained and definitely not thinking straight. It just felt as though we had to do something to protect Charlie. To protect all of us.

"I'm sorry," I murmured as I rested my head down on my arms. "You're right."

"We don't know who's right. All we can do is hope it's the right choice," Ryder said resting his hand on my knee.

The room fell silent. I couldn't stop thinking about what had happened to Charlie. If she hadn't caught me with Ryder, none of it would have happened.

I wanted to know how Ryder found her, but I imagined he'd followed her footprints in the snow. He'd probably gotten very lucky, and then lucky again when the snow let up so that they could find their way back.

We sat there in the dark shivering. Shawn watched out the windows as best as he could. I knew how hard it was to see in the dark. If he saw anyone, it would probably be too late, but of course, I wasn't going to remind anyone else of that fact.

"Why don't you try to get some rest," Ryder said patting my hand.

"OK," I said, entwining my fingers with his. "Come with me?"

He nodded and laid down next to me. Logan guided Charlie over to the spot on Ryder's other side. She curled up into a ball, and Logan covered her.

Charlie's back was to Ryder and I. Her body trembled so much I knew there was no way she could be sleeping. She hadn't liked me, and I can't say I was particularly fond of her, but I never would have wanted anything bad to happen to her.

"If I ever see them again... I'll kill them," Ryder said, mostly to me. His eyes were unfocused. I could feel his anger rising as he was likely thinking about what he'd seen. "I'll never forget their faces."

"They're probably long gone," Charlie said as if she was disappointed he couldn't come through on his promise.

I hoped she was right. I hoped they weren't determined to get her back. They could be hanging around nearby just waiting for an opportunity to take her away.

It wasn't like they were finding new women to torture on a daily basis. If they wanted her badly enough, they might come back.

I tried to push the thought from my mind, but I couldn't. I kept visualizing them out there in the darkness, watching us.

I wouldn't be sleeping. Not tonight.

"We should leave in the morning," I said resting my head on Ryder's arm.

"Maybe," he said. "Go on, close your eyes."

I looked away so he wouldn't see me staring into the darkness. I'd be surprised if any of us would actually fall asleep after everything that had happened. But I needed to be ready. I was the one with the gun.

23

The sun was shining. Droplets of water fell off of the icicles that decorated the exterior of the windows.

After we finished off what was left of the wolf, we packed up, which hadn't taken long. Charlie stood near the door soundlessly rubbing her fingers together.

Logan peered out of the window in the front while Shawn stared out the back.

"All clear?" Ryder asked.

"Clear," Shawn yelled, and Logan nodded.

"Everyone ready?" Ryder asked, looking first at Charlie and then me.

"Yes," I said.

Charlie gave a shaky thumbs up.

I closed my eyes as he opened the door, not because of the bright sunlight but because I half-expected to be ambushed. Thankfully, what was in my imagination, hadn't happened.

It was hard to walk through the deep, wet snow, but no one complained. It was melting, and that meant it was getting warmer. No one talked as we plowed our way through, but that seemed to be our new normal.

I couldn't shake the feeling we were being followed, but it must have been all in my head. There wasn't a soul in sight. We could see for miles around us... no trees and no buildings, except for the one we were leaving behind.

It was just us, the snow, the sun, and sky. No one could sneak up on us without being seen, but that didn't help ease my mind.

It was hard leaving behind the house. While it wasn't safe to stay, it was a roof over our head. If it started snowing again, like it had been, we'd be in major trouble. The house had saved us. What were the odds of that happening again?

We marched through the snow for hours without coming across any living creatures. Maybe everything was dying out. The only tracks in the snow were ours in the snow behind us.

"Anyone need to stop for a rest?" Ryder asked.

Further ahead a small square shaped structure popped into view. It was hard to tell at our distance exactly what kind of building it was, but it appeared to be leaning to the side.

"No," Charlie said. The snow crunched as she stomped her boot down into the snow.

"OK, we keep going then," Ryder said when no one else spoke up.

I glanced at Shawn to make sure he was doing OK. It hadn't been that long ago that he'd been in rough shape.

He flashed me a smile as he moved his legs up and down through the snow. It was hard to believe he was even the same person I'd found lying in the snow, close to death.

Something over his shoulder caught my eye. I tilted my head forward trying to look around him. Shawn squinted before he turned to follow my gaze.

There were black dots peppering the distant sky. I wasn't sure if they were the same big black birds we'd encountered or if they were different, but there seemed to be more of them. They'd gathered reinforcements.

Either way, I knew what they were capable of. Any amount of them were too many as far as I was concerned.

"I don't think they see us," Shawn said, and Ryder cranked his head to see what he was talking about.

"Shit," Ryder said, reaching out towards Charlie for her club. Her face was tilted down. She must have been deeply lost in her thoughts because it didn't even seem as though she'd noticed anything was going on.

"It doesn't seem like they are coming this way," I said watching them as they got smaller and smaller.

It didn't take long before I couldn't even see the little dots in the sky. I was glad they hadn't come our way because none of us were in any condition to deal with the birds. Shawn and Charlie both still had their bandages from the last bird confrontation.

As we approached the decrepit slanted shack, we walked by cautiously. The area was empty, but there was a circular area where the snow had been melted away. It looked as though there had been a fire burning there, not that long ago.

Ryder pulled off his glove and stuck his finger into the black ash in the middle of the circle. He stared at his fingers while he rubbed them together.

"It's cold," he said.

"They would be in minutes at this temperature," Shawn said, his eyes on the shack. The door creaked as it swayed back and forth slightly.

Logan's pink fingers wrapped around the handle of his knife, and he pushed the door open. His head moved as he scanned the space inside. "There's some wood piled up. Otherwise, it's empty."

"Should we take some?" I asked wondering how much I could fit in my backpack.

Ryder and I each stuffed a log into our packs. "Too heavy?" Ryder asked as he pulled on his pack. "Logan could—"

"It's fine," I said with a smile. It wasn't that I didn't trust Logan with my things, I did, but I felt more comfortable carrying it myself.

"Let's get out of here then," Ryder said. "In case whoever was here comes back."

We didn't delay to move out of the area, but we weren't more than twenty feet away from the shack when I saw movement out of the corner of my eye. Or at least I thought I had.

I tugged at Ryder's jacket sleeve, but when I tried to focus on where I'd see something, there wasn't anything there. Perhaps it had just been my imagination.

"Never mind," I said, straightening my shoulders. Ryder studied me for a moment before shifting his gaze forward.

I stared at the area, I'd thought I'd seen something. I almost laughed at myself. There wasn't anything there except for drifts of white snow.

Wait.

Tracks.

Were those tracks?

I was almost certain.

My hand shot up to Ryder's arm again as something whizzed through the air off to my right. I looked around as my heart pounded hard against my chest.

"What is it?" Ryder said noticing that I'd stopped moving.

"What was that noise? Are those tracks?" I said short of panic. I pointed toward a pile of snow that had gathered in one area. The wind had caused snow drifts, they were everywhere since we'd left the house.

Ryder started walking to where I had pointed to have a closer look. I grabbed the back of his jacket and pulled him back. Something was wrong. I could feel it.

"Let's just keep going," I said taking in a sharp breath as something grazed my leg just below the knee. "Oww!"

It felt like something had stung me. I bent down and touched my leg. I must have walked into something that had been buried in the snow and scraped my leg.

When I raised my hand up, I saw the blood on my glove. Ryder's eyes widened.

"Are you OK? What happened?" he asked, his eyes darting around the area before shifting down toward my injury.

"I must have walked into something. It feels like something stung me," I said examining the ground around my foot. There wasn't anything there. At least not that I could see.

That was until something in the snow caught my eye. A couple feet away from where I stood, something was poking out of the snow.

I took two steps closer, avoiding putting too much weight on my hurt leg. When I realized what I was looking at, my breath felt as though it was caught between my lungs and my mouth. It squeezed my throat.

"Arrow," I mumbled and turned around to face them. "We have to get out of here."

Ryder followed my gaze and looked at my leg. His eyes widened as something zipped inches past his arm. "Run!"

24

I t was nearly impossible to run in the snow. What we were doing, was more like a fast, awkward march.

I turned and looked behind us, just as one of the snow-covered, camouflaged men stood up and aimed an arrow at us. It looked as though he'd had a cloak made from a white wolf, the wolf head over his head like a hood.

I only saw the one man, but the arrows that came our way seemed to indicate that there were others. Even though I tried, I couldn't tell where the others were hiding.

I pulled out my gun, but I couldn't use it while we ran. My bullets were limited. I couldn't waste them, not to mention I didn't even know how many guys were out there, or where they were.

"They're camouflaged," I said between breaths.

With each step I took, warm blood seemed to stream down toward my ankle. The impact of my foot stomping into the snow sent a stinging jolt through my veins. My lower leg felt as though it was being torn in two.

Charlie was out in front, leading the way. She was being fueled by an intense fear.

Her arms abruptly jerked up into the air. Charlie lost her grip on her club and it flipped end over end before sinking into the snow. Her body flopped forward, and she fell face first towards the ground.

"Ugh!" she grunted.

"Was she hit?" I asked in a high-pitched voice as I glanced around frantically. I didn't see the camouflaged man, but something told me he was still there.

Ryder inspected Charlie and pulled her to her feet. He looked into her eyes. "You're OK. You're OK."

"I tripped," she said, her eyes bugging out of her head.

There was movement to my right. Shawn was next to me, so I grabbed his arm and pulled him down to the ground with me. The arrow landed and stuck into the ground several feet in front of our faces.

They were after us. They weren't going to give up.

"At least they seem to have terrible aim," Shawn said with a weak, fear-filled chuckle.

He was right. They must have known it too, because with us on the ground, they got up from their hiding spots and ran toward us.

"They're coming!" I warned, scrambling to get to my feet.

There was one thing they were good at, and that was moving through the snow. We started to run, but they'd caught up.

One of the guys after us jumped past me and landed on top of Ryder, knocking him to the ground. My feet slid into the snow, and I came to a stop.

I pushed the guy with both hands trying to get him off of Ryder. The guy jerked his elbow back, hitting me square in the chest knocking me away. The weight of my backpack pulled me down, and I grunted when I hit the ground.

Logan started toward Ryder as another guy caught up with us. It looked as though there was something in his hand as he popped Logan on the back of the head. His steps slowed as his eyes rolled back into his head and he fell forward.

Charlie screamed.

Shawn had got up and ran over to fight off the guy that had hit Logan. He launched his fist at the guy, striking him so hard blood sprayed out of his nose.

Ryder threw his fist upward and smacked the guy on top of him in the throat. The guy didn't even hesitate to punch him right back.

I reached back and pulled out my gun, attempting to aim it at the guy moving around on top of Ryder. When Charlie screamed again, it broke my focus.

"Help me!" she cried, desperation soaking her words.

A third guy wrapped his arm around her middle and pressed his hand down over her mouth. He started dragging her away.

Three guys.

I wiggled out of my backpack and aimed up a shot as I took big steps in Charlie's direction. A hand wrapped around my leg, and I stopped. Fingers dug into my wound.

Whoever had me, jerked my leg back, and the last thing I remembered falling face first toward the ground.

25

My body rolled forward slowly and then gently rocked back. I was on the beach near our home with my dad, watching the waves gently slosh over the sand.

Water splashed against the sides of the small dock. The wetness in the air was so thick I could taste it. I looked over my shoulder and into my dad's eyes.

He smiled at me. I felt safe. I felt happy.

"Wake up," he said, his voice soft. I smiled back but felt confused by his words. I was awake.

My body started to rock quicker, and my dad's expression changed. He looked worried. A darkness I'd never seen filled his eyes.

"Get up, Emery!"

"What's wrong?" I asked, but before I'd finished my sentence, he fizzled away. The waves were gone too. The world around me shattered like broken glass leaving me encapsulated by nothing but a freezing, white cloud.

My heart was pulsating aggressively at the back of my neck. The coldness made me shiver, and my eyes fluttered rapidly.

"Emery! Wake up!" Shawn was looking at me as he shook my body vigorously.

"My head," I groaned trying to sit up.

Shawn wrapped his arms around me and helped me sit up. "You were hit."

"Where's Ryder?" I asked looking around.

"Behind you," he said. It took effort, but I turned and saw him cleaning his knife in the snow. The still wolf-hide covered man laying on the ground lifelessly at his feet.

Logan was pulling himself up out of the snow. He rubbed the back of his head while he looked around. "What happened?"

"You were knocked out," Shawn said.

"They took her," Ryder said.

Logan stood up but wobbled so severely he fell down to his knees when he couldn't balance himself. "We have to go."

Ryder nodded as he pointed at the snow. "They went that way. We have to hurry."

"I don't see them," I said looking out toward the horizon. There wasn't any sign of them except for the boot prints in the snow. "How many were there? Three?"

"Yes, just three, I think… well, now two," Ryder said kicking the body on the ground. "This was the one… I came through on my promise."

"Now we just have to get her back," Logan said, back on his feet. "Otherwise it won't even matter."

I started to cry. Shawn held me even though I could tell he didn't know why exactly I was breaking down.

I hadn't been out in the world as long as the others had, but I knew it was hopeless. We'd never be able to find her… not in time. Would she even be able to survive whatever they were going to do to her?

They all stared at me. "She could already be dead."

Ryder swallowed and nodded. "I don't think so. They could have just done that here if they wanted to. I think they want to keep her."

"They've already put her through hell," I said unable to stop the tears. "They'll do it again."

"Can you walk?" Ryder asked looking at me and then at Logan.

"Yeah." I sniffed, as I tried to pick up my backpack. Thankfully they hadn't bothered to take it. Shawn reached over and grabbed it from me when he saw me struggling.

He slipped it over his good shoulder. "Just temporarily. When you want it back, let me know."

I nodded, but the movement made me feel dizzy.

Logan moved his feet, but he weaved side to side as if he were intoxicated. "Go," he growled, his face plastered with frustration. "Let's go get her."

I looked up at the sun and then at the tracks in the snow. The world started to spin.

"What's wrong?" Shawn asked looking at me when I didn't move. I stared at him, but I couldn't say anything. He grabbed my shoulders and looked into my eyes before turning to Ryder. "I don't know if she's OK. She was hit pretty hard."

I blinked slowly. "I'm fine."

I wasn't.

It felt like an imaginary string was pulling me south. If I turned and followed the footprints, it would break. I'd be lost.

I had to decide.

There wasn't time to spare.

South like my mom said... or help my new friends? My dad's warnings flooded my mind. How had this happened?

My heartbeat was like a ticking clock.

Tick.

Tock.

Tick.

Tock.

26

I sucked in a deep breath and closed my eyes. My heart was pounding so hard it felt like it was going to explode inside of my chest.

"OK, ready," I said swallowing hard. I sucked in a quick breath that froze at the back of my throat threatening to choke me. "Let's go."

My heart didn't stop pounding as we headed west. The string between me and the south pulled tighter and tighter. I tried to ignore the fact that I was finding it harder to breathe.

It was easy to follow the tracks in the snow, at least for the time being. I wasn't sure what we were going to do if we lost them, but I wasn't about to ask.

Ryder was walking so quickly that he was actually quite a bit ahead of Shawn and I. We could still see him, and really that was all that mattered.

Logan was in between, sometimes he'd be closer to

Ryder and sometimes closer to us. His weaving around had improved but based on how often his hand was on his head, I knew it must have still hurt where he'd been hit.

Ryder turned around and waved at us aggressively. He said something, but I couldn't make out what he'd said. It was difficult, but I tried to walk faster.

My leg still hurt where I'd been hit, and I was suffering from a major headache I was trying to ignore. The pain I was in was hard to hide.

"You OK?" Shawn asked.

My teeth were clenched, and I was sweating despite the cold. "I don't have a choice not to be."

Shawn's eyes shifted down toward my leg. I didn't want to look. If I saw it, I'd be tempted to stop. It was better if I didn't even know what it looked like.

"They could go ahead," Shawn suggested.

I bit my lip. "I don't want to get separated."

"No, right, of course not."

When we caught up to where Ryder had been when he'd waved at us, I noticed what he'd been waving about. There was blood sprinkled in the snow, leading in the same direction as the footprints.

"Must have been the one I'd hurt," Shawn said.

"Or maybe they're hurting Charlie." I sniffed.

The sun seemed to be moving quicker than it had earlier. It would be night soon. We had to find Charlie before it was too dark to follow the trail.

Logan had caught up to Ryder again. I hated how

far ahead they were from us, but I knew time was of the essence. It was frustrating because no matter how fast I walked it didn't feel like I'd ever catch up.

I tried to make my feet go faster, but when they didn't do what I wanted them to, I tripped over my own feet. Shawn caught my arm and steadied me before I fell into the snow.

"We'll catch up to them," Shawn said, making sure I had my balance before letting go. "They won't lose us. I won't let them."

The sun was even lower. Each step to the west seemed to make it inch lower and lower toward the horizon.

"Time's running out," I blurted. "She didn't even like me."

"Only because of him," Shawn said.

I shook my head. "I don't think so. She didn't like me the minute she saw me."

"She's a tough cookie," Shawn grinned. "That's how I know she'll be OK."

"You can't possibly know," I glanced at him, my brow wrinkled.

Shawn stiffened his jaw. "You're right. I don't know, but if anyone would survive them, it would be her."

Maybe he was right, but what he wasn't factoring in was that this time they were taking her after they'd already broken her down. I didn't know if it would be possible for her to get her hard shell back up in time to survive whatever they were dishing out.

Bits of snow shot up from their boots as Ryder and Logan started running. Shawn pulled my arm.

"They see something," Shawn said squinting. "It's them!"

———

I watched from afar as Ryder leaped on top of the guy that was holding Charlie. All three of them tumbled to the ground. The guy lost his hold on Charlie, and she scrambled to get away.

The second guy started to go after her, but Logan dove toward his foot and tackled him. Charlie screamed as she looked around, not knowing what to do.

Shawn waved his hand at her, but her eyes were wide. Charlie was panicking and had no idea we were even there.

"I'll go get her," Shawn said handing me my backpack. "Watch your back. Scream if you have to."

I nodded, and he ran off. The pain in my leg seemed to increase, but I kept walking. If I could get closer, I could help.

Ryder rolled on top of the guy he was fighting and hit him in the jaw. He pulled back and hit him again.

I was about ten feet away when I reached back for my gun. My fingers moved around as I frantically tried to find it. Nothing was in my waistband.

It was gone.

I turned around, my eyes darting in every direction as I scanned the ground. Had I dropped it?

I turned back to see Logan staring at the man he'd been fighting. He was holding my gun to the back of Ryder's head.

"Get off of him," he screamed, droplets of spit spraying out from between his teeth.

Ryder raised his hands. Shawn and Charlie froze in place.

The guy must have taken my gun after he'd knocked me out. He hadn't cared about my supplies, just my weapon.

I noticed Charlie's hand were empty. My eyes quickly scanned the ground.

About halfway between the guy with the gun and me, was Charlie's club laying in the snow. One of the bad guys must have dropped it when Ryder charged them.

I took a step forward, and Shawn's head jerked to the side. His eyes warned me not to move.

If the guy holding the gun spotted me, it was over. But if I could get to the club without them noticing....

I took another cautious step.

"I said, Get off of him!" the guy said pressing the barrel to Ryder's skull.

"OK! OK!" Ryder said shaking his hands.

The guy on the ground sat up, but he hadn't seemed to notice me through his swollen eyes. I took another step.

Five more steps to the club.

Five more after that to reach the guy holding my gun.

Ryder got up slowly. His eyes moved around slowly as he was taking in the situation. He spotted me but quickly shifted them away.

Step.

"Stand by your friend," the guy with my gun said quickly turning around and spotting Charlie. "Both of you. Over there."

Another step.

Charlie clung to Shawn as they walked over to Ryder and Logan. The guy with my gun kept his back toward me as the gun followed their movements.

Step.

Step.

"Here's what's going to happen," he said alternating who the gun was pointed at.

The guy with the puffy eyes, and a bloody lip stood up and squinted in my direction. He rubbed his eyes.

Dammit.

Step.

I bent down low to the ground and grabbed the club. The guy with swollen eyes tapped his buddy on the side of the arm and whispered something.

I gripped the club tightly and charged the guy holding my gun. He slowly turned and aimed the gun at me.

I was less than three feet away when he pulled the trigger.

27

I ducked even though I wouldn't have ever been able to dodge the bullet. The guy holding the gun hadn't realized the safety was still on.

I raised the club over my shoulder and swung as hard as I could. He cried out when the nail-spiked club hit him in the shoulder.

His fingers spread apart and the gun dropped into the snow. He reached over trying to take the club out of his arm. I snatched up my gun and made my way over to my friends.

The guy with swollen eyes turned to run, but Logan grabbed him before he could get away. Ryder stepped up in front of the guy who'd tried to shoot me and ripped the club out of his arm.

The guy howled out in pain, his eyes rolling around in their sockets. It looked as though he was going to pass out, but before he could fall, Ryder pulled back the club and aimed for his head.

I closed my eyes, but I heard the squishy thud upon impact. Shawn started to lead both Charlie and me away. Even after we were a good distance from the scene, I still didn't want to open my eyes.

"You save bullets this way," Shawn said as if he was trying to explain. I nodded, but that didn't mean I'd wanted to see any of it.

Charlie was on his other side sobbing almost silently. "The fuckers deserve it. Same guys. I'm glad their dead!"

"What was that?" Shawn said jerking his head back.

Over my shoulder I saw Ryder and Logan running towards us, waving for us to keep going. I could tell something was wrong.

"Go, go, go!" Shawn said pushing at my back until I limped forward in an awkward run.

Seconds later I'd heard the distant mumbling voices. We weren't far away. Nowhere near far enough.

"Hey! What happened here?" one of the voices said.

The sun dipped below the horizon wiping out the last bits of light. I turned back, but I couldn't see anything. In fact, I could barely see Ryder and Logan.

Someone screamed, and another wailed loudly. They were going to catch us.

"Keep going," Ryder said grabbing my backpack. "As fast as you can."

"It doesn't matter," I said between breaths. "They'll see our tracks."

I looked down and barely noticed the path we'd taken to find them. It was hard to see in the dark, but it was there.

"We have to switch directions. Maybe they'll follow the wrong set," Shawn said.

"Follow me," Ryder said and turned off in another direction.

We didn't stop running even when we couldn't hear them anymore. I wasn't sure if I'd ever stop running.

We'd probably been running at varying speeds for an hour straight when a sharp pain stabbed in my leg. A reminder of where I'd been hit by the arrow.

"My leg," I said unable to catch my breath. "It hurts."

"All right, we can slow down." Ryder looked concerned even though he hadn't seen my leg. "Hopefully, we'll hear them coming."

Logan muffled a cough. "Hopefully."

Ryder glanced at my leg. "How bad is it?"

I shrugged. "I don't really know. It kind of burns."

"Is it bleeding?" Ryder asked.

"It was."

I didn't want to look because it felt like a chunk of my flesh was missing. It probably needed to be bandaged, but I didn't want to stop and take care of it. We needed to keep moving until we were safe. If that was even a possibility.

"I wish there was a way to cover our tracks," Shawn

said as he slowed and tried to kick snow over our deep footprints. It wasn't enough to make any real difference.

"We just have to hope they aren't following," Ryder said. "And if they are, we need to be moving faster than they are."

"How many were back there," Shawn asked.

Ryder pressed his lips together briefly. "Not sure. Ten? Twenty?"

Charlie exhaled loudly, gesturing in the direction they had been dragging her. "I think their home was back that way somewhere. One of them had said we were close. They said that soon I wouldn't have to worry about The Evolved anymore."

"They didn't know you were a renegade?" I asked.

"No, and I didn't tell them. Would it have mattered?" Charlie asked.

Ryder shook his head. "Probably not. Renegades are just The Evolved's rejects. At least that's what the natives think."

"And the natives are the rejects of both," Logan quipped.

"Shh!" Shawn said, and everyone stopped talking. The world around us was completely silent. After a few moments, he shook his head. "Sorry, I thought I heard something."

"Well, did you?" Ryder asked.

Shawn drew in a deep breath and exhaled slowly. "No. Nothing. I'm fairly certain."

"We should probably stop talking anyway," Ryder said his eyes peering into the darkness. "It's not like we want to draw any unwanted attention to ourselves."

Logan chuckled softly. "Is there such a thing as wanted attention anymore?"

Ryder smiled. "No, probably not. Especially when it comes to the natives or The Evolved."

We walked in silence for a long time. No one made any noises. The only sounds that could be heard were the rustling of our clothing and our boots in the snow as we walked.

After a while, Ryder leaned in close. "That was a little scary back there… and actually quite brave."

"Some would say it was foolish," I whispered. "I'm lucky he had no idea how to use a gun."

"I'd be willing to bet a lot of people don't have experience with them. We just don't see them around much anymore," Ryder said.

"Do you know how?" I asked.

Ryder looked over his shoulder. "Not well."

I shrugged as I reached back to feel my gun tucked back into my waistband. It felt good to have it back. "Well, hell of a lot of good it did me."

"Maybe not this time, but it could."

"That club is going to do us much better than my gun ever will."

Ryder shook his head. "I'm not sure if that's true. The club is useless against those arrows."

"My leg says the gun was pretty useless too."

"I'm just glad you're OK. I don't know what I would have done if—"

"Thankfully we don't have to talk about it," I said.

Ryder squeezed my hand and kissed the side of my head. It was almost too hard to believe that we were still together and still alive.

I was sure the others were still thinking about Eli. It was hard to keep going on without him, but what choice did we have? Eli would have wanted us to keep fighting.

We walked until the sun came up. There wasn't anyone behind us that we could see, of course, that didn't mean they weren't still trying to find us. But at least we were ahead of them, and hopefully, it would stay that way.

We stopped for a short break to eat something and drink some water. I cleaned my wound as best as I could and bandaged it. It wasn't as bad as I had thought, but it still hurt like hell. The arrow had grazed my skin and ripped off a small chunk of the upper layer of my skin. There was a big black bruise around the wound, but it would heal.

As soon as we were finished with our rations, we were back on our feet. I looked up towards the sky at the white clouds drifting by. The welcomed sunlight was warm on my skin.

The good news was that we were headed south again. Hopefully, the snow would melt, we'd replenish our supplies, and before we knew it, we'd be organizing our new home.

All we had to do to make it our reality was avoid the natives and The Evolved until we got there. How hard could that be?

This is the end of Book One in the Ravaged Land: Divided series.

Sign up for my mailing list to be one of the first to find out when book two is released.

If you enjoyed this book you may also enjoy the Ravaged Land Series.

- - - - -

Thank you for reading! If you liked this story, please leave a review!

BOOKS BY KELLEE L. GREENE

Ravaged Land: Divided
The Last Disaster - Book 1
Book 2 Coming soon!

Ravaged Land Series
Ravaged Land -Book 1
Finding Home - Book 2
Crashing Down - Book 3
Running Away - Book 4
Escaping Fear - Book 5
Fighting Back - Book 6

The Island Series
The Island - Book 1
The Fight - Book 2
The Escape - Book 3
Book 4 Coming Soon!

The Alien Invasion Series
The Landing - Book 1
The Aftermath - Book 2

Destined Realms Series
Destined - Book 1

MAILING LIST

Sign up for Kellee L. Greene's newsletter for new releases, sales, cover reveals and more!

COMING SOON...

Book two in the Ravaged Land: Divided series is coming soon. Please subscribe to the mailing list to be one of the first to know when it's available! And follow Kellee L. Greene on Facebook.

ABOUT THE AUTHOR

Kellee L. Greene is a stay-at-home-mom to two super awesome and wonderfully sassy children. She loves to read, draw and spend time with her family when she's not writing. Writing and having people read her books has been a long time dream of hers and she's excited to write more. Her favorites genres are Fantasy and Sci-fi. Kellee lives in Wisconsin with her husband, two kids and two cats.

For more information:
www.kelleelgreene.com

Made in the USA
Coppell, TX
27 January 2023

11789407R00142